Be you!

Always!

# Backslide

## NICOLE DYKES

# QUICK NOTE

There are some things in this book that may trigger a person who's had past trauma. I never, ever want to hurt with my words. The only things I ever want to do is heal, strengthen, and hopefully, just hopefully, promote change in a world that can truly be ugly.

There are side characters who—because I hate the word homophobic. (I agree with the memes that you aren't afraid of gay people, you're just an asshole)—refuse to change and are ugly, nasty people. And there are also characters who don't even realize or recognize the ugliness and hate they have inside themselves.

I don't enjoy writing these types of characters, but I do try to write books that are extremely real. And unfortunately, those people do exist in this world. In the end, I hope this book brings you joy and gives you a sense of triumph because in the end . . . I truly believe the good will win over the bad in all things.

*Your Betrayal*

**Bullet For My Valentine**

*What You Make It*

**With Confidence**

*Remedy For Reality*

**Real Friends**

*All Away*

**Happydaze**

*Wanna Be (feat. Machine Gun Kelly)*

**Jxdn**

*Catching Fire (feat. nothing, nowhere.)*

**Sum 41**

*July*

**Noah Cyrus**

*I Want More*

**KALEO**

*Bruises*

**Lewis Capaldi**


*Arcade*

**Duncan Laurence**


*Take What You Want*

**Post Malone**


*Set Fire to the Rain*

**No Resolve**


*After Rain*

**Dermot Kennedy**


*Angels Fall*

**Breaking Benjamin**


*Killing Me Slowly*

**Bad Wolves**


*I Will Not Bow*

**Breaking Benjamin**


**I don't own the rights to any of these songs. But these are the songs I listened to over and over as I wrote this book because each one felt like they had a connection to Nash and Adrian.

# Nash

"WHY ARE you staring at me like that?" I ask as Hayden's eyes roam over the entire length of me. It's warm for early November, and we've been working out in the hot sun, trying to get the tenth cabin built before the Christmas rush.

My younger brother and his wife, Raelynn, bought this land and four rundown cabins two years ago, and after fixing up the fourth cabin, they wanted to add more. With my background in construction, they invited me to come and help them.

I was more than happy to help. Lawson, my brother, has always been a priority in my life, even before he ran off from Texas to Missouri with Rae. She was in trouble, and he was hellbent on saving her.

I was an asshole about the whole thing. I couldn't see past my love for Lawson to realize Raelynn needed help. So maybe I'm here to make amends as well as for the steady work. They offered me part of their business, but I don't want it. I'm more than happy just living in one of the cabins free of charge and receiving a steady salary as "the help," as Lawson so lovingly refers to me.

Hayden is a guy around Lawson and Raelynn's age they picked up along the way on their journey out of hell. He was living on the streets, like they were, when they met. He's a partner in their business now, and I have to admit he's grown on me over the two years I've known him. He has a smaller build but has filled out from these last couple of years of hard labor, building cabins and chopping firewood for the bonfires and fireplaces, which are part of the amenities included with staying in the cabins.

"You just look like every single jock that beat my ass in high school," he says, gesturing toward my body, "with your shirt off and bulging muscles on display. I'm not sure if I should be turned-on or terrified." He shakes his head. "What a way to go, though, if you do kill me for drooling."

I roll my eyes and pick my shirt up off the ground. It was hot, and I was sweating, so the shirt isn't comfortable. I frown in his direction. "Why would anyone beat you up for drooling?"

He snorts and picks up a hammer, starting to work again, looking away from me. "Please. Big, straight man." He stops hammering and gestures to himself. "Skinny, totally gay twink. I was a hot target."

I feel a growl bubble up my throat at the thought of anyone hurting Hayden, but I know his life was no picnic, growing up gay in the deep south. It's why he ran away from home long before he became an adult.

"That's some bullshit." I steady the board he's working on. "And who said I was straight?"

He turns his head, gaping at me. "What?"

I shake my head at him and nod toward the nail. "You gonna finish that?"

"Are you telling me—after two years of mild flirting with the man I thought was straight—I actually have a chance? Because that's the real bullshit."

I laugh at him, amused because he is a flirt. But Hayden will flirt with anyone, including women, who he has zero interest in actually bedding. "You never asked if I was interested in men. You assumed."

His jaw may actually be touching the ground. His big eyes widen even further. "You are shitting me."

I take the hammer from him and pound the nail into the wood. "Why would I joke about that?"

"You're gay?"

I grab another nail and place it but don't lift the hammer as I face Hayden, who's still comically surprised. "No."

"Asshole," he snaps, looking haughty. I can't hold back the laugh escaping from me.

"I'm not sure what I am, Hayden. I've been with women before." He scoffs, folding his arms and staring at me, waiting for me to explain further. It's not really something I want to go in to. "But I've been with a guy too."

"A. Guy? As in one?"

I feel my tension building, thinking about that one guy. "Yes."

"Once?"

I groan and shake my head. This is why I've never brought it up before. I know Hayden pretty well by now, and there's no way he's letting this go. I blame the sun baking my brain for letting it slip. Or maybe it was him assuming I'm like the stupid-ass, homophobic guys from his high school. I don't know.

"No. It was more than once."

"You're fucking with me. I know it. This is so not funny."

"I'm not fucking with you." I finish placing the nails in the board, keeping it secure, and then put the hammer down to face Hayden. "I was with one guy several times. So, I'm definitely not totally straight, but I've enjoyed being with women too."

Random hookups throughout the years to chase away the loneliness. I don't know why I haven't been with another man since then. I try not to think about it too much and chalk it up to convenience in the small conservative town I grew up in. And I'm not one who really needs a lot of company. I've always been a loner, more satisfied with quiet calm than boisterous chaos.

"What happened with the guy? Did he ruin you for other men?" He leans in, way too excited. "Was he just that fucking good? Or was he that bad? Did he break your poor, sweet heart?"

I snort and move over to one of the camping chairs we have set up for our breaks. "My heart is not sweet. And something like that."

3

He takes the seat next to me, his hand poised on his knee as he leans in, salivating for more information. "Okay, I need more details."

I shake my head, my hand absently going to my heart as I rub the spot. "No."

"Naaash," he whines, and again, I laugh because Hayden is just easy to like.

"No. It was a long time ago. I was a kid. So was he. It's over."

*So damn over.* "How does your brother not know this? Or has he been holding out on me? The bastard."

"Lawson doesn't know about it. No one really does. It's not a big deal."

"It made you leave dick behind. It must have been a big deal."

I shake my head at him and turn away, looking at the cabin we've almost finished. "It did not make me leave dick behind. I just . . . I haven't been attracted to another man since. I've been busy."

He scoffs. "Um, hello? You aren't attracted to me? I'm a catch." I turn back to him, and his face is filled with fake offense.

I tell him the truth. "Hayden, you're a beautiful man, but I see you as another little brother."

"Fucking ouch." He grabs his chest as if he's wounded.

"An adorable little brother," I add.

"Double ouch." He waves me off and stands up. "Fuck you. I'm hot."

I'm not kidding, Hayden is beautiful. Beyond gorgeous. But I really don't feel anything sexual in connection with him. I do feel a strong sense of protectiveness toward him though. "I know." I stand up and pat him on the head. He shoves me away playfully, barely budging my bigass body.

"Listen, if you want to make it two dicks you've played with, the offer is there."

I ignore him and walk back over to the tools. "We need to get this done. It's hot today, but by the end of the week, it'll be cold."

"Way to change the subject." He walks closer and mumbles, "At least then you'll keep your shirt on."

I laugh, "You like me without my shirt."

He groans and then shakes his head slowly from side to side. "I really, really do."

"Stop."

"You started it!" he squeals, and I hand him a hammer, ready to get back to work.

*And to keep all my thoughts off that one guy.*

"So, really just one?"

I sigh in exasperation. "Hayden . . ."

"What? I'm just saying—"

"I know," I interrupt him. "It just hasn't happened."

It's been a few days since I let it slip that I've been with a man before, and Hayden has, of course, not dropped it for very long since. I love the kid though. "But why?"

"I don't hook up that often, and it just so happens when I have, it's been with a woman. It's really not that big of a deal."

"I can't believe it."

"Can't believe what?" Lawson walks into the dining room right on time with Rae behind him. They both look drained from working on a different cabin than Hayden and I have, but both are smiling too.

Hayden's eyes meet mine in a silent apology, like we've been caught in some great big secret. But it's really not that. The only reason I haven't told Lawson about being with a guy before is I just don't talk about hookups with my brother. Or anyone. I'm usually tight-lipped. But Hayden can make anyone talk.

"That I haven't been with a guy in a long time."

Lawson's eyes widen slightly, and Raelynn grins oddly knowingly. Raelynn looks at Hayden. "Oh my God. Of course, you're obsessing."

He shoves her playfully. "Shut. Up."

"You're gay?" Lawson asks, no malice or disgust in his voice. Just curiosity. Which isn't surprising, considering he's a good man and Hayden is his best friend. Still, the town we lived in—grew up in—was enough to poison anyone.

"No." I shrug my shoulder, not wanting any of it to be a big secret but not really knowing how to label myself either. Labels are fucking stupid anyway. "I've been with one guy and some women. I'm attracted to both, I suppose."

"Wow." Lawson's lower lip pokes out as he processes that. "I always thought you were a monk, but Rae said you had to be hooking up occasionally."

"It would be a fucking sin to let that body go to waste," Hayden interjects.

Lawson shoves him playfully and laughs, "Quit drooling over my brother."

"Yeah. That's never going to happen, especially now that I know one Davis brother loves cock."

"Sounds like he's a fan of cock *and* pussy," Law says, and I cringe, not a fan of talking about my sex life.

"Okay. Let's talk about something else, for the love of God." I plop down at the table in the dining hall we also built. It's where we put out the complimentary breakfast buffet for guests, but it's where the staff eats all our meals.

Rae takes a seat next to me, looking pretty damn excited. "So, we just booked something pretty amazing!"

"What?" I raise an eyebrow in her direction, knowing it must be big with how excited she is.

"Four cabins for two months."

"The same party?"

Lawson nods as he sits down across from me. "Yeah. Some senator's son or something and his fiancé. Or something. I don't know. I didn't pay much attention after they said they wanted four cabins for two months and there will be publicity."

I scratch the hair of my beard, thinking it's probably time for a trim as I lean back in my chair. "High profile guests, huh?"

Rae nods. "Yes. So, we have to make sure the cabins are ready.

They'll be here next week. And the new ones are the best ones, more luxurious and all that."

They've gone all-out in building the last cabins. "That should be no problem. I think we'll be finished with the one we're working on in the next couple of days."

"Good. This could be huge for us." Law has that hopeful look in his eyes I'm so damn glad he has now. There was a time when he didn't expect anything to get better or go his way. No matter how much I tried to shield him from our parents, who were addicts and just plain lousy most of the time, he's seen plenty in his short time on the planet.

"It'll be great."

"Thanks, Nash. I knew we could count on you."

I preen a little at that compliment from my little brother. Even though he's only five years younger than me, we've had more of a father/son relationship, and I want nothing more than for him to be happy.

"So back to you liking dick." We all groan in Hayden's direction, and I pick up a dinner roll from the middle of the table and toss it at him.

We all laugh before settling down for dinner.

*I'm not big on high-profile types—too self-important to give a damn about other people—but if this will help make Law and Rae's place more successful, I'll do whatever I have to do to make these guests feel as comfortable here as possible.*

# Nash

"OH MY GOD! They're on their way!" Raelynn tears through the dining hall where the guest also check in, apparently making sure everything is in its correct place. But she looks like a lunatic.

"Sweetie, you're acting like a nut." Tammy says this. Not me. Tammy is another Texas recruit. She was Lawson's friend before Rae moved into our small town, and she's now Rae's best friend. And she's pretty much the only person who can calm Rae's ass down.

"I want it to be perfect," Rae tells Tammy, but she finally stops for a minute and stands still.

"All the cabins are finished," I supply.

"That's right because we're badass." Hayden parks himself next to me, wearing his forest-green Davis Cabins polo and khakis. I hate our uniforms, but I'm wearing mine today as well. I know how important it is for Rae. "And all the custom, organic fucking goat-milk soap is in all the bathrooms."

Raelynn loves the farmer's market here. Lawson wraps an arm around her and kisses her temple. "It'll be perfect."

She nods. "The son. The senator's son, who's also in politics, is dating one of the top travel bloggers in the world. I mean, this could make or break us."

"I thought it was his fiancé?" Hayden never misses a detail.

Raelynn shakes her head at him. "No. Lawson doesn't listen to details, but I did my research. They aren't engaged yet, but her father is also a senator. It's like some kind of goddamn political royalty we have staying here for two months! And she'll be blogging about her time here."

She's right. This really could be huge.

"We'll make it a great stay, Raelynn," I try to assure her, but I can see her nervousness about this. She wants this to work out. She wants it to be a success. I get it. Rae was born into wealth. She walked—or rather ran—away from it because her stepfather was an abusive asshole. She chose a life with my brother on the streets over being owned by her parents. Raelynn is fierce, but she wants success.

It's in her blood.

And Lawson and I will make damn sure she gets it.

"Nothing will go wrong." Lawson stares into her eyes with intensity. I have to look away but hear him say, "I promise you."

He loves her. No statement has ever been truer. He could have had a full ride to college—the kid is the most talented artist I've ever seen. But he gave that up and ran to keep her safe.

And God, I want this to be a success for him too. I want them both to thrive and maybe prove there is true love out there that can conquer all. I've seen it with them. I've never experienced it for myself, but I know it's real when I look at them.

I hear Rae take a deep breath and then the jingle of the bell on the door. We all turn as several well-dressed people walk through the front door. An older man with salt-and-pepper hair and dashing good looks is the head of the party, and his voice is deep and commanding. "We're here to check in for the Walker party."

*Walker.*

Raelynn stumbles toward the front desk, and I think the poor girl is trembling as she tucks her hair behind her ear. "Yes, of course. We're so pleased to have you here."

The man offers a smile—but it's practiced. "Fantastic, dear. We're thrilled to be here as well. Thank you for accommodating us for such a long stay."

Rae is smiling, but her nerves are strong. I'm worried she may faint. "Of course. We have four cabins ready to go. The numbers are on the keys." She hands them to him. "Our staff will be happy to lead you to them."

She gestures behind her to Tammy, Lawson, Hayden, and me. Hayden has his bright smile on full display, and Tammy and I are trying our best. The man looks us over and gives a quick nod. "That would be lovely." A slender woman with hazel eyes that seem oddly familiar to me sidles up next to him. "This is my wife, Mary. And I'm Theodore, but you can call me Theo. Or Senator Walker." He winks as if that's a joke.

I've gone numb. I recognize them. Memories I've pushed away are barreling forward with a vengeance.

Rae laughs, but it's the polite kind of laugh. "Absolutely. It's nice to meet you."

The senator signals someone behind him to step forward. "And this is my son, Adrian."

*Fuck. No. Shit.*

All the air in my lungs leaves me as he wraps his hands around broad shoulders, and his son's face comes into view. It's a beautiful face framed by perfectly styled, dark blond locks and a pair of hazel eyes I've stared into many times.

*No.*

"It's nice to meet you." He must notice her nametag. "Raelynn."

That voice. It's deeper now, but it's the same. Goosebumps form on my arms. "It's wonderful to have you here."

"This is my girlfriend, Samantha." A gorgeous, leggy blonde steps up next to him with a bigass smile on her face, and I notice Adrian's arm is around her slender waist.

She holds out an elegant hand for Raelynn to shake, and they make small talk about the cabins and the area while I try not to lose my shit.

*How the hell is he here? Why isn't he in Texas?*

While his girlfriend charms Rae and his parents, Adrian's eyes start to roam around the room, and I feel the exact moment he sees me. I think my knees might not hold me up. His eyes widen as he takes me in, his lips part slightly as my heart slams into my ribcage over and over.

I want to run. I want to run the hell out of here and never come back, but I stay in place. Schooling my features to not give away my freak-out, I don't acknowledge him. And he doesn't acknowledge me.

He merely goes back to the conversation before they introduce the remaining guests that consist of the assistants, and a decision is made that the fourth cabin will be for Samantha's parents, who will arrive tomorrow.

*This cannot be happening.*

*Adrian*

T<small>HIS IS NOT HAPPENING.</small>

*How is he here?*

*Nash Davis.* After all this time. He's here in my presence during this shitshow of a "vacation." This can't be happening.

But it is. I know it's him. Even though it's been a good seven or eight years since we've been in the same room. I feel woozy as I try my best to listen to Samantha and my dad go on and on about activities in the Ozarks and how beautiful it is here.

My eyes keep drifting back to Nash. His eyes won't meet mine. But they're eyes I've memorized, eyes that haunt every unconscious moment and live in my mind, maybe even my soul.

He was always tall, a few inches taller than me, but he was lanky. Now he's all hard, compact muscle. His biceps strain the fabric of his sleeves, nearly splitting them. His dark hair is a little longer on top, unruly and wavy, and he's sporting a full beard now.

I need to look away. I cannot keep staring at him like this.

"Well, we can't wait for that." I'm pulled back to the conversation when Samantha loops my arm with hers and is smiling in my direction.

I know my role here. I'm supposed to agree even though I missed the subject. I nod my head at the pretty brunette behind the counter. "Sounds great."

Samantha is beaming, but I can't tell if this is her public persona or the real her at this point. I'm pretty sure the two are intertwined now. Don't get me wrong, her ambition is one of the things that drew me to her in the first place, so I don't fault her for wanting to make her blog the best it can be. And with ten million followers, I'd say she's been pretty damn successful.

"We should go and get settled. Right, Adrian?"

Again, I agree and let her lead me from the dining hall and outside, sneaking one last glance at Nash. Thankfully, my father declines a personal escort and instead, just takes directions from the woman —Raelynn.

When Samantha and I go into the cabin we'll be staying in, my heart still races as I'm bombarded with so many memories, I'm afraid I'll drown in them. Samantha wastes no time pulling her phone out and snapping pictures. "This place is the cutest."

Yeah, I can't breathe. Let alone talk.

*Nash. How the hell is he here?*

"Are you okay? You look pale." Samantha approaches me as I try to steady myself against the front door of the cabin.

"I'm fine. Jetlag."

She snorts and waves that off quickly. "Right. You travel all the time. I've never seen you look like this."

I want to plead with her to let it go, but I know her too well. We've been dating for three years, and she's never let anything go. "I'm fine."

"Do you not like it here?" she asks, walking away from me and sitting on the sofa in the living area of the cabin.

I need to get it together. If Samantha tells my mother, she will, no doubt, tell Samantha's mother, who will tell *her* father, who will go back to *my* father, and I'll be royally fucked. Because that's the way it goes.

My father is always trying to save face. We're not allowed to look messy or tarnish the reputation my great-great grandfather built. We are Walkers.

I rake my fingers through my hair and drag in the air I desperately need before walking over to sit next to her. "Of course, I do. I'm just tired. I don't think I slept well."

She grins at that, turning to give me her best pout. "Well, if you'd have let me relieve a little of your stress last night, maybe you'd have slept better."

*Keep it together, Adrian.* I force a smile onto my face. "I'm sorry. You're probably right."

She stands up, phone in hand again. "You work too much."

I drag my hand in the direction of her phone. "You're one to talk, sweetheart."

She giggles at that and then plops down next to me, holding her phone up and placing a poised kiss against my cheek as the flash nearly blinds me. I'm used to it by now. I, Adrian Walker, am part of her brand.

*And I hate it.*

*All of it.*

I want to rip the tie from my neck and the stupid suit jacket off my shoulders and scream out to the world that I'm over this life assigned to me by birth. But as she posts the selfie to her social media, I know that'll never happen.

Because I'm a coward and always have been.

I stand up and glance around the cabin. It's nice. They said it was handcrafted on the website. It seems professionally built but definitely with care. I go into the bathroom and see the large glass shower and all the usual amenities. I quickly splash water over my eyes and dry my face with a soft, green towel before I stare at myself in the mirror.

I'm a piece in the game for my father. I always have been. His one and only son. Heir to a throne I never wanted. And now, I'm here in the Ozarks, trying to close his final and greatest deal. My marriage to Samantha Foster will tie two powerhouse political families together and help the men at the heads of the families become even more powerful.

Senator Walker and Senator Foster, a match made in conservative hell.

"You sure you're okay?" I look over at Samantha, at her silky smooth skin that's on display now that she's removed her coat and is wearing a black sleeveless dress and heels. In the Ozarks.

"Yeah. I'm sorry I worried you." I turn off the bathroom light and press a quick kiss to her lips. "I'm going to go for a walk, okay?"

"Okay, great. I'm going to do a live intro to our cabin." She barely notices me as I leave the cabin, already gearing up for her live stream. And I'm grateful for it.

I walk down the path leading down to the lake and away from the cabin, but I stop quickly, my feet not moving as soon as my eyes zone in on Nash speaking to another employee. His eyes meet mine with the same fire and fury I expected.

*I'm glad he hates me.*

*He should.*

# Nash

"ARE you going to talk to me or what?"

I try my best to focus on Hayden, but all I can seem to concentrate on is Adrian, who's standing all alone, looking at me. "What?"

Hayden huffs, "Nash, you look sick and have since the Walker/Foster party walked in." His eyes assess me, making me shifty and uncomfortable. "I mean, their politics suck, but Rae's right about them being good for the cabins."

My jaw tightens, thinking about Theodore Walker. I can't believe I didn't recognize him right away. His political ads have made me want to vomit so many times over the years. When I left Texas, my first relief was not having to see them when I turned on the television. He's aged since then but is still as handsome as money can buy.

And he has plenty of that.

"Nash." I can hear Hayden's worry.

"No, it's fine. I'm fine. I just want this to go well for Rae."

He's still studying me, but thankfully, he seems satisfied. "I looked up Samantha Foster when I was researching the other political douchebags."

"You mean in the ten minutes since they've been here?" I'm amused by him. I can't help it.

He holds up his phone. "Yes. Of course." I see the Instagram account he's showing me, and the first picture is of the pretty woman and Adrian in their cabin. They look carefree and comfortable with

19

each other. My stomach rolls, but Hayden must not notice. "Samantha has over ten million followers, and she's going to be posting about this trip. This could be fucking huge for the cabins."

I try to force a smile, but I know it's more of a grimace. "That's great."

"It is." He's beaming as he places his phone in his pocket. "So, we have to do our best."

"We will." I see Adrian is still staring at me, imploring me to talk to him. I hate that I can still read him. That I can feel his desperation wafting toward me. I clear my throat and focus on Hayden. "Can you do me a favor and grab Law to start gathering firewood? Rae wants to go all-out for the bonfire tonight."

"Yeah, okay. What are you going to do?"

*Don't look at Adrian again.* "I'll be right there. I just need a minute."

He shrugs and thankfully, for once, doesn't fight me. He just pats my shoulder and then is off to find Lawson. I take a deep breath of the now cool, fresh air and then stride toward Adrian, praying my legs won't give out as they tremble.

He meets me in the middle, his hazels boring into me with intensity that quickly turns to fury as we meet, and he hisses, "What the hell are you doing here, Nash?"

I'm taken aback for a minute by the hostility dripping from his tone. "Me? What the hell are *you* doing here? I thought you'd still be in Dallas."

"I live there. I'm . . ." He's flustered. Which is far different from what I remember of him. Adrian Walker was always perfectly poised, ready for anything that was thrown at him. He straightens his tie—because of fucking course, he's wearing a goddamn tie out in the middle of nowhere—and then drops his hands. "My father rented out this place for a couple of months. My fiancé's father recommended it."

"Fiancé?" I'm taken aback by that. I thought they were only dating.

"Oh, fuck." He's flustered again. His clean-shaven cheeks turning pink from the cold air and annoyance before he runs his fingers through his golden hair. "No. Not fiancé. Not yet anyway." His hand falls back down to his side. "Look, don't mention that to anyone."

"Fine. I couldn't give a fuck." And I couldn't. I swear.

He snorts, annoyance pouring from his pompous-ass self as he moves in closer to me. "No one here can know . . ." At first I think he's still talking about his impending proposal, but then he falters, his body stiffening as his eyes flick around the area around us. He must be satisfied that no one is near because he continues, "About us."

"Us?" I cock an eyebrow, folding my arms over my chest. "There is no us." My tone is cold and angry but collected and calm.

"You're damn right there isn't." His hazel eyes meet mine, and I see the desperation I remember. The fear. The need to keep me hidden. Along with himself. "But just in case you have it in your head that there ever was . . ."

I drop my arms and take a step closer to him, crowding him, towering over him even though I only have a few inches on him. "In my head." The words are a thick growl because how fucking dare he?

I watch his elegant throat flex with a tight swallow. "Yes." His hazels plead with me for a brief moment before he clears his throat, squares his shoulders and schools his features back into politician mode. "I'm assuming you aren't going anywhere."

It's not a question. "I live here. My brother is the owner."

He processes that and then nods. "Don't breathe a word of our . . ."

I lift an eyebrow, waiting and not giving him any sort of reprieve. "Past."

"Past." The word feels bitter on my tongue as I spit it out.

"Yes." The tendons in his neck stretch tight. "Past. What we had . . . What we did . . ."

"Was nothing," I bite out, not wanting to hear what he was going to say but fairly certain it was something similar.

"Two kids. Stupid mistakes."

Movement catches my eye, and I nod in the direction of his cabin. "Your fiancé is waiting."

He turns to look over his shoulder at the blonde, who is watching us with quiet curiosity, and then his eyes meet mine. "My *girlfriend*. Samantha Foster. Daughter of Senator Paul Foster."

As if that's supposed to mean something to me. I don't pay

attention to senators anymore. Or really anything political. It makes my gut tighten, just thinking about the fake bullshit that goes on. The pleasing smiles. The fake promises. That shit I now know runs through Adrian's veins.

"Right." I'm still assuming she will soon be his fiancé though, considering his earlier slip. That this whole trip is about that—the merging of two political families. *Oh, the headlines.*

He straightens his coat and stands stiffly, unmoving. "Not a word, Nash." His eyes darken ever so slightly as he tries his hand at a threat. "Or you'll be sorry."

I lean in, unable to stop myself, inhaling his expensive cologne and attempting to force away all the feelings trying to claw their way to the surface from that one whiff. "I'm not the same boy I once was, and I don't hide from anything now. There's nothing you can hurt me with because I know exactly who I am. I stand here, and everywhere I go, firmly okay with every part of me."

His eyes search mine, and I can tell his breathing has sped up like mine has. We stare at each other. So many words left unsaid. So much pain under the surface of the shit we did to each other.

*He's my greatest regret.*

*I'm still his biggest secret.*

# Adrian

I CAN'T CATCH my breath. *Jesus fucking Christ. Why does he have to be here? Why does he live here?* I force myself to go back to my cabin where Samantha is waiting for me. "Who was that?"

"Staff," I make myself say.

"He's gorgeous."

Fuck. Leave it to Samantha to state the obvious. "I wouldn't know."

Her laugh is light and flirty as we walk back inside the cabin. "Oh, come on. You can admit another man is good-looking. And I wouldn't begrudge you from looking at the female staff." She waggles her perfectly manicured eyebrows at me, and I snort a laugh.

"I was just asking about the farmer's markets around here. Thought you might want to go."

She squeals at that like I knew she would and hops on the couch, curling her legs underneath her. "Oh, what did he say?"

*Didn't think that one through.* "Uh, he suggested we search for it."

Her nose crinkles, and her lips pout. "Well, that's not the kind of service I'd expect."

*Great. Now I'm tanking his brother's business. Could I be more vile?*

His words echo in my head.

*"I'm not the same boy I once was, and I don't hide from anything now. There's nothing you can hurt me with because I know exactly who I am. I stand here, and everywhere I go, firmly okay with every part of me."*

*Does that mean he's out now? Is he with someone?*

23

The thoughts are not helping my breathing situation. "Are you okay?"

I finally yank my tie off and sit next to her on the sofa. "I'm fine. He was friendly. He gave me directions, like I asked for."

She shrugs her shoulders at that, leaning her head against the sofa. "Well, Raelynn was super friendly. Speaking of that . . ." She leans in closer, her fingers working the top button of my dress shirt open. "Apparently, they're having a bonfire tonight to welcome us. We'll have to change."

I see that look in her eyes and know she's interested in more than just removing our clothes and putting on more appropriate ones for outside. But there's no way I'm in the mood for that now, not after seeing Nash.

After speaking with him. Hearing his voice. Looking into those eyes.

I stand up. "I need to make a call first."

"What?" She's pouting hardcore now. "A work call?"

"Is there any other kind of call?" I shoot back, removing my coat. "It won't take long."

"Adrian." Her voice reflects her disappointment. "My father thought this would be a great vacation for us and time away from work."

Actually, her father, along with mine, thought this would be the perfect time for me to finally pop the question. She grew up in this state, and they frequently vacationed in the Ozarks. Her father planned all this for me to propose in a grand way that will have her followers screaming. And I guarantee neither he nor my father will be here for very long. Both are workaholics.

"He's not here."

She climbs up from the couch, one hand poised on her hip. "You know he will be. He promised. I've been worried about him."

My tone softens along with my entire attitude because he had a heart attack last year. It was mild, and they kept it out of the press, but I know it frightened Samantha. And her mother. Hell, maybe even Paul, although he hasn't slowed down since. And I know his promises mean shit. Why Samantha still believes a word he says, I'll never understand.

But I'm not one to talk. I know my father is full of shit, and yet I'm still at his beck and call.

I place my hands on her slim shoulders. "I'm sorry. I promise it will be a wonderful and relaxing time. There are just a few loose ends I need to tie up."

Her bottom lip is still slightly protruding, but she nods her head in acceptance. "Okay. I'm going to try to find a suitable outfit for the bonfire. I can't wait to take a pic."

"There's my girl." I kiss the tip of her nose, and she giggles softly before bouncing into the bedroom.

I pull out my phone and connect with the office, going over a few necessary things before finally hanging up just as she leaves the bedroom, dressed in a purple oversized sweater and black leggings, matched with high boots. "What do you think?" She does a spin for me.

"You look great." I stand and join her near the entrance to the bedroom. "I'll get dressed, and then we can go."

Her hands slide over my chest, and she grins coyly up at me. "I think we have time to break in the bed first." She bites her bottom lip, and my eyes scan her pretty face. She really is stunning. Flawless skin. Pink, full lips. Small, slender nose that most women would kill for. I want that flicker of passion to flood through me. I want to feel the desire I should feel.

But I close my eyes slowly and see dark eyes, a beautifully cut jaw now covered by dark hair. Red lips poking out from that beard and strong, bulging muscles that flexed tight as he yelled at me.

I was such an asshole, but it was better that way. I need him to hate me, to hold on to that feeling just enough so he stays away but not so much that he decides to tell everyone here everything.

*Do I really think he would?*

I don't know. He should be angry, and part of me wouldn't even blame him, but I know Nash. Deep down, he's loyal. I don't think he'd ever do that to me.

I open my eyes and put on my best practiced smile for Samantha. "Wouldn't want to get you all messed up before you get a chance to take your picture."

She shrugs at that and nods as if it makes perfect sense. She's just another piece of all this. Her parents aren't thrilled that she chose blogging instead of going into politics, but she's successful in her own right—so they deal with it.

Our marriage, popping out a few kids to continue this line of perfect, beautiful people—that's what her father really wants though. And she plays the game as well—if not better—than I do.

"Get dressed." I turn toward the bedroom, and she playfully smacks my ass. "I don't want to be late."

I go into the room and strip out of my suit, finding khakis and a douchebag sweater she picked out for me. I suppose this is my casual wear for the night. I put it all on, and we get our coats on before she slings her arm through mine, and we head outside into the cool evening air.

I see the girl I know is named Raelynn from her nametag, standing with a handsome man who must be Nash's younger brother. His arm is wrapped around Raelynn's waist, holding her to him in a protective pose that still gives her freedom to laugh and joke around with a stunningly handsome man with a slight build and beautiful eyes full of playfulness. I saw Nash talking to him right before our confrontation. Nash stands with them, and the man ruffles his hair, causing Nash to pull the much smaller man into a playful headlock and do the same to him.

*Is that his lover? His boyfriend?*

Inexplicable jealousy rushes through me. I'm not sure if it's because he's able to be who he is out in the open or if it's the thought of Nash with another man. But I find I've stopped walking in their direction all the same.

"Are you coming?" Samantha looks over her shoulder in my direction with a questioning gaze.

I nod, but my feet won't move. I stay there, watching the scene before me. Nash is smiling. Happy.

Not that I've never seen his smile before, but this seems different. He's different now.

"Adrian." The sharp snap in Samantha's voice pulls me from my stupor, and I drag the zipper of my coat up higher and nod again.

"Of course. I'm sorry."

She smiles and takes my hand, pulling me toward the bonfire and the man I once had . . .

*Or could have had . . .*

*But I'll never have again.*

# Nash

*Why does he have to be here?* I want to be different now. I want to be stronger. I don't want to be affected by his presence in the slightest.

But when he approaches with his perfectly put-together, beautiful soon-to-be fiancé, I feel like I might die. Like all the air in my lungs has left me and is never coming back. He offers a friendly smile as Raelynn jumps into host-mode and introduces Hayden and then Tammy as she makes her way to the bonfire with hotdogs and supplies for s'mores in tow.

I offer to take some of it from her, and she gives me a smile before allowing me to help her. I need to keep my attention off Adrian. I can't think about him or what he was to me at one time. That was a long time ago.

I was a different person then. Fresh out of juvie and feeling so totally lost. He came crashing into my life then, literally running into me in the halls of our high school our senior year. His father thought it would be good for him to spend his last year of high school out of his fancy private school and around "normal" kids.

So he transferred to our public school and arrived late his first day. Terrified he was going to let his father down even then. It should have been a red flag, how high-strung he was about being late on his first day. But instead of walking away like I should have done, I tried to calm him, placing my hands on his shoulders and leading him to his class. I even gave him my number in case he needed anymore help from me.

I should have walked away and never looked back at the well-dressed kid with beautiful, sparkling hazel-green eyes so full of worry. But I didn't then. I will now.

"Do you think Rae got enough?" Tammy asks, looking at all the food and laughing.

I grin, knowing Rae went overboard but loving that about her. "Should be."

Tammy and I start grilling the hotdogs, using sticks Rae bought for that purpose while Rae, Hayden, and Lawson play hosts, greeting the senator and his wife. The rest of the staff either isn't allowed to join or is currently working because it's only four guests at the moment.

And I would kill for more people to be here so my eyes would stop drifting to Adrian. He stands stiffly next to Samantha when his father approaches him, and his mother stands at his side. All in a perfect line, picture-ready.

And it seems Samantha can sense it's the perfect time for just that because she hands her phone to Raelynn, asking her to take a picture. Rae complies, snapping the moment and handing her phone back to a happy Samantha, who instantly examines her phone.

*Is that really what Adrian wants?*

I try to push away the thought. I don't give a good goddamn what he wants.

But my eyes meet his through the haze of the fire and the chaos of everyone trying to get dinner ready. Everything stills around us when we lock gazes. His shoulders are pushed back as he stands stiff as a stone next to Samantha. He's numb.

But his eyes are screaming.

*Does anyone else around him notice?*

*Do they care?*

I force myself to look away. Not caring. I don't care anymore. I can't.

"Nash." I look over at Tammy just as she nudges me with her elbow. "I think it's done."

"What?" I look at the hotdog currently charring to a crisp in the fire. "Shit." I pull it out of the flames and stare at the charred remains.

Tammy stares at me, looking amused. "You okay?"

"I'm fine." I toss the ruined hotdog and work on another one, more carefully this time. Trying to ignore Adrian and everything his being here has brought up.

My first kiss with a boy. My first everything with a boy. My first heartbreak ever. And my last. I haven't allowed myself to get close to anyone since Adrian.

I stop the train of thought before I burn this hotdog, and we serve up plates to the guests before grabbing our own plates. The senator and his wife spend quite a bit of time staring at their hotdogs before finally diving in.

This is far from their usual meal, that I'm certain of. Adrian, though, is not looking at his plate. He's looking through the fire. At me. Studying me. Way more than he'd like, I'm sure. But I see him.

*I've always seen him.*

# Adrian

"Son?"

*Shit. What was my dad saying?* I have to stop watching Nash. What we had was nothing. It was less than a year. That's it. A blip in time. Nothing.

I don't know who the man sitting across the fire from me is anymore. I have no idea what he likes anymore. *Does he still have an oddly adorable obsession with comic books?* And not the normal Marvel or DC comics. No, he liked off-brand, unique ones.

*Is he still ticklish only on his right hip?* The strangest thing. He can take being tickled everywhere except for that spot.

*Does he still pay his mom's bills?* Even though he lives here?

*Does he still live with the weight of the world on his shoulders?*

"Adrian?" *Right. Dad.*

I pull my gaze from Nash and look at my dad. "I'm sorry. What were you saying?"

His forehead creases with the disappointment I'm used to from him. "I said my plane leaves tomorrow morning."

That grabs my attention. "What? You're leaving tomorrow? We just got here."

He straightens his shoulders, looking at me as if I'm still a child. "We both know I can't stay here long. I have responsibilities, Adrian."

Right. Playing the political game. Public appearances and behind-the-door deals. All so very important to Theodore Walker. "You're not even staying for twenty-four hours?" I look over at Samantha, who's talking with Raelynn about God knows what. "I thought this trip was important."

I straighten my own shoulders in a mock position, but it gathers no respect from my father, who only scoffs. "I don't see Paul here either."

"Samantha said he'll be here soon."

He chuckles, but it's humorless as always. I don't think I've ever heard an actual laugh from my father. "I'll believe that when I see it. I know he's in D.C. as we speak. And I doubt he'll be able to pry himself away for at least a week. He has some important meetings this coming week, and I need to be there as well."

*Important.* He loves that word. Along with *responsibility*. And *appearances.*

My jaw tightens, and I try to take a deep breath before I snap. Because Adrian Walker does not snap. He's calm and collected. Always.

"Then why are we here? If there's work to be done?"

His eyes grow even more serious as they meet mine. "You know exactly why you're here. You don't need me to hold your hand. You know the objective."

*Objective. Another word he loves to throw around.*

A derisive snort erupts from me before I can stop it. "How romantic."

He stands from his seat and directs me to follow him with his head. I stand also, knowing he thinks I'm dangerously close to making a scene. My eyes catch Nash's only briefly before I follow my father further away to receive my lecture. When we're far enough away, he turns his body to look directly at me. "This is not about romance, Adrian. You know that. I know that. So why even pretend? This is serious, and you need to start acting like it."

Everything inside me is screaming at the top of my lungs.

*That I hate him.*

*That I hate this life I'm stuck in.*

*That I don't want this "objective." To marry a woman I'm not in love with.*

*That a proposal shouldn't be a fucking chore. An objective. A marriage shouldn't be a political merger.*

Although I'm screaming all of that deep inside, my face remains passive. No one would know any of that. "And you and Paul don't want to be here for that?"

"Of course, we will be. It will be at Christmas dinner, like we discussed."

*Right.* The great proposal plan that Paul and my father came up with together. Alone. Not with me. I wasn't involved at all. They told me what was going to happen, and I agreed. Like I always do. I follow the plan. I tow the line. I'm the perfect son.

He places a hand on my shoulder, his eyes deadly serious. "And until then, you and Samantha are having a fairytale vacation for the ages. She can post it all to her silly social media page, and they can all fawn over how perfect you two are. They're watching us, Adrian. Always watching us."

"I thought you didn't approve of her career?"

He laughs, but it's almost evil. *Dismissive.* "Career? Please. But there's no denying she has quite a reach, and as long as she stays in line, it's beneficial." My stomach rolls, listening to him. One time, and I mean one time only, Samantha caught a picture of two men holding hands at a resort where we were staying. There were other couples in the picture, mind you, but it didn't matter.

Those two men in her picture—two men who looked truly in love —set off a fire storm. She had to apologize publicly for "ruffling any feathers." She didn't want to. Despite her upbringing, she's not a terrible human being, but to her father, she was hurting his reputation as a conservative, family man with "values."

The whole thing makes me sick to this day. That's what my father means by "staying in line." By only posting "good, wholesome pictures." And I hate him even more for it. I can't say anything, and I can barely look him in the eyes.

"Of course, when you're married, the whole travel thing will end.

But she'll still retain her followers, I'm sure. She'll just have to shift her focus."

That gets my attention because this is something we haven't discussed yet. "Samantha loves to travel. Her followers live through her experiences."

Another dismissive snort. "That's really quite pathetic." I glare at him, standing there waiting for more, when I know I should run away. I should just fucking run. But I don't. "They will love her new life after you're married. That of a beautiful wife of a politician. She can post about that. And when you have children, she can be an example to all the women out there."

"To be a quiet wife, right? That's all women are for? To sit there and look pretty?" My tone has a distinct bitterness to it. How can anyone ever vote for him? How can they look at my parents' marriage and think this is what they want?

"Stop. This is no time for your feminist bullshit."

I glare at him, unmoving and silent like the coward I am.

"Now, we can discuss this more in the future, but you know Paul has hoped she'll stop this traveling nonsense for a long time. If he can't get through to her, it will be your job as her husband to do so." He starts back toward the bonfire, and I follow, my legs doing what they always have—just like the rest of me—they follow.

He grabs my shoulders when we stop closer to everyone. "Hug me."

"What?" I'm sure I look as horrified as I feel at his request.

His jaw is tight with tension, losing patience. His voice is quiet when he says, "Hug me, and say goodbye." His eyes dart toward the people around us quickly and then move back to me as he pulls me in for a big hug. One that makes me physically ill as I stand stiffly in his arms. His voice is much louder and more jovial than I've heard in private from him. "I know you'll take care of everyone while I'm gone, son. I can always trust you."

I catch my mother's eyes over my dad's shoulder. She tilts her head to the side in a practiced movement, looking at us adoringly as if we're a father and son with a real relationship. As if it isn't all fake.

He releases me, and I fight the urge to vomit on him as my eyes catch Nash's. He's watching me intently. He sees right through all the bullshit.

*He always has.*

My father pats my shoulder and then walks to my mother, Samantha, and Raelynn to say his polite goodnight before he retires to his cabin. And when he's gone, I flee.

I escape deep into the woods because it's too damn much.

I don't want anyone to follow. I don't want to face the world. I want to disappear.

I want to scream.

But all I do is stop at the edge of the lake and stand. I stare.

*And I think about being anyone else, other than the person I am.*

*Nash*

DON'T FOLLOW HIM. *Don't. There's no reason to follow him.*

But my dumb ass doesn't get the memo. After Adrian's father and mother go to their cabin, Raelynn, Samantha, and Tammy settle around the fire to look at photos. Hayden and Law start cleanup, and it's like no one realizes Adrian is gone.

I follow him, my body on autopilot like that's what it's supposed to do. Like it remembers from all those years ago. Get to Adrian.

*God, I'm pathetic.*

I find him at the edge of the woods, overlooking the lake. He's just standing there, totally unmoving.

"Are you going to jump? Because it's pretty fucking cold."

He slowly turns to look at me, his shoulders slumped in defeat. But he doesn't seem surprised. "Why are you here?"

"In Missouri? In the Ozarks? You'll have to be more specific." I'm an asshole. He's clearly broken, but I don't care. I can't care anymore. *He broke me. He deserves this.*

That's what I keep telling myself over and over.

"You can't save me, Nash."

I scoff at that and take another step in his direction. "I don't want to."

He doesn't miss a beat. "Then why are you here?" He seems to remember my previous statement and adds, "At the lake. Right now. Why did you follow me?"

That's a good question, one I don't have an answer for, and he knows it.

He shakes his head at me and sighs, "Go away, Nash. Go back to your beautiful boyfriend."

That catches me off guard for a minute. And I don't know what he's talking about until it clicks a moment later. *Hayden. He has to be talking about Hayden. Is he jealous?*

*Do I care if he is?*

No, I decide. And I try to convince myself of that.

"Hayden is doing fine without me for the moment." Yeah, I'm a total asshole.

His face morphs into something I can't quite pinpoint. His eyes move behind me briefly and then back to mine. "Hayden."

I nod. "The beautiful boy."

"Right." His shoulders straighten now, his chin lifted in cold defiance. "Go back to him, and stay away from me. I meant it when I told you to stay away earlier, and still, you follow me mere hours later?"

"You're a guest. You looked distressed. It's my job to check on you." It's bullshit, and we both know it.

He snorts, "Right. I'm fine, Nash." There's the Adrian I know. Stubborn. Defiant. Afraid.

"You're not fine."

I saw the way his father was looking at him. I saw the sick look on Adrian's face as he listened to whatever hateful things his father was saying. He's anything but fine.

"You don't know me anymore, Nash. I am fine. I'm here with my *girlfriend*." The word is said with so much bitterness.

"Right. Your girlfriend."

"That's right," he snaps defensively. "Now go back to your boyfriend and leave me the fuck alone. We can't be alone together."

I step closer to him, too close because once again I catch the scent of his cologne. "Why not? Huh? We're just two men, staring out at the lake." I gesture widely with my arm toward said lake to make my point.

He looks pained now. His eyes never leaving mine. "That's not . . . Stop."

It's pleading. His voice. I've heard it before. Asking me to kiss him and then to *not* kiss him. To never tell anyone about us. To stay with him. I've heard that tone from Adrian Walker so many times. And it still guts me to this day.

"Stop what?" I move closer to him, his body a magnet for mine even still. And when I'm only a foot away he puts his hand up to stop me from coming any closer.

"This. Stop. Do not follow me. Don't check on me. Hate me, Nash. Hate every single thing about me."

"I do."

He shakes his head, and his shoulders droop yet again. "You don't. This is what you do, Nash."

"What the hell does that mean?" I instantly become defensive, my body stiffening.

"It means you're a savior. You have to save everyone. Your mother. Your brother. Me." If I could set him on fire with my eyes, I'm pretty sure I would as my glare deepens.

"Don't talk about my family."

"That's right, Nash." He doesn't look away. He boldly holds my gaze, daring me. "Hate me. Get angry and stay that way. I'm not your family. I'm not anything to you."

"I didn't say you were."

Again, he looks like he's in agony as his eyes bore into mine in the moonlight surrounding us, bouncing off the lake water. "I'm the boy who left you standing all alone. Who lied and killed a piece of you." His mouth moves to my ear, sending a shiver down my spine at the close contact. His voice is raspy as he breathes his words, "Don't you ever forget it."

He steps away from me then, leaving a cold emptiness throughout my soul.

"Go back to the bonfire. Go enjoy your boyfriend. He's stunning."

Part of me is shocked he admitted that another man is beautiful out loud, but it's not like anyone else is here. I want to correct him.

Tell him Hayden isn't my boyfriend, but his words stick straight into my heart. He was the boy who left me all alone like an idiot. I thought he loved me. I thought we were going to ride off into the sunset together, but he never showed.

That's who he is. And I need to remember it.

My face morphs into a cruel smirk. "That he is. Can't keep all that beauty waiting."

I spin around to leave, but his words catch me before I can. "Nash."

I look at him over my shoulder. "What?"

"Be discreet."

*He. Did. Not.*

I turn fully and walk back toward him so fast my world nearly spins. "Be discreet? You just said those words to me? I told you I don't fucking hide anymore, Adrian. There's no way in hell I'll hide him. Or anyone. I would never do that to someone."

He rears back like my words stabbed through him, and I'm glad. I feel an odd satisfaction. Because fuck him and him making me hide for a damn year. For making me feel ashamed of my feelings. For confusing me and making me bitter and angry. "I just mean—"

"I know exactly what you mean," I cut him off. Clenching my hands into fists at my sides and trying not to throttle him. "I. Don't. Hide."

"I didn't mean that." He looks over my shoulder, back toward the cabins. "I mean, if my father or my mother see you openly out with Hayden . . ."

"You think I give a flying fuck what those closed-minded assholes think?"

"You should."

Yeah, I might hit him. I'm not usually violent. Despite my big, badass exterior, I don't like fighting. "I should?" My teeth are clenched so tight it nearly hurts.

"Yes. Listen to me, you stubborn jackass."

*That's it.* I step forward, our shoes touching and glare down at him. "I'm the stubborn jackass? I see right through you, Adrian. You've forgotten, but I know how much your father disgusts you. How his politics make you want to fucking puke. I know you. Don't you dare act self-righteous with me."

"Listen. To. Me." His voice is back to that pleading tone. "They chose this place because it's . . ." he huffs and looks around, taking a step back from me, "wholesome."

I snort, a sickening feeling deep inside overtaking me at that word. A word that is supposed to mean having values, and yet it's been changed into "as long as you have the same values as me." And it's disgusting.

His eyes close briefly, and I know that word has the same influence on him. That he hates it just as much.

*Goddammit, why does he go along with this shit?*

"If they see you with him. If they know you're gay . . ." My heart is thumping wildly in my chest as I wait. "They'll make Samantha destroy you. Your brother's cabins. We'll leave immediately."

"You're really threatening me?"

He shakes his head slowly. "I'm warning you." His voice is quiet and defeated. A soft sigh in the night. His gaze meets mine. "Be careful."

"If they did that, we'd have just as much support afterward. People would flock here just to give those homophobic assholes the finger."

"I wish that was true, Nash." His voice is still quiet, and I try to fight all the memories of our time together. Of the quiet nights in the back of my truck, looking up at the stars. When no one else was around and he was being who I thought was the true him, his voice was still so damn quiet.

As if he was afraid someone would discover him, even out in the middle of nowhere.

"They'll ruin them."

Fear I haven't felt in a long time sweeps through me. I've gotten used to being me. To watching Hayden be himself openly wherever we went. To being free. When you're surrounded by good, it's easy to forget there's really, really bad out there.

He brushes past me, and I just barely catch his words. "I don't want them to."

He disappears, and then I'm left out by the lake. All alone.

*Once again.*

# Nash

MY BODY IS STILL THRUMMING with anger and pent-up disappointment from the past. We were young, but I thought what we had was real. It happened so damn fast. Our first kiss was in my car when I gave him a ride home.

I'd never felt that way about a guy before, or really anyone, but I knew I wanted to kiss him. It was like I was consumed with the need to kiss him. And when I did—there were so many emotions flowing through me. I was worried he'd be grossed out. Or hell even hit me. Or tell everyone at school. As far as I knew, there was no one else in our small school like me.

All the boys our age were busy chasing girls. Talking about girls. Dreaming about girls.

Not that I didn't. But the day I laid eyes on Adrian Walker—he was all I thought about. His blond locks that were cut short. His hazel eyes that sparkled in the sun. His sharp jawline and lean muscles. He was all I wanted.

And when my lips finally touched his, it was as if my entire life before that moment didn't exist and nothing else mattered. I didn't even care if he ended up punching me in the face. But he didn't. He let out a startled gasp against my lips, and then his fingers were in my hair, pulling me into him. Kissing me back with a heated intensity I'd never felt before.

But when it was over and we were both struggling to catch our breath, that's when I saw the fear in his eyes. That's when his gaze darted to the front of his house—even though I was pretty sure no one was home. He was home alone a lot.

And that's the first time he told me that no one could ever know about what happened. The first time he asked me to hide a part of me. And I, in a complete and total daze, agreed. I wanted to keep him safe from whatever it was he was afraid of, and hell, I felt my own kind of nerves too.

"Nash?" I'm snapped out of the past when I step through the thick woods and back toward the fire that's started to die down, and I hear my brother's voice.

"Where is everyone?" It's only Lawson out here now.

"The senator and his wife went to their cabin. Rae, Tammy, and Hayden are cleaning up the dining hall. And Samantha said something about going 'live.' Whatever that means."

*Hell if I know.*

I grunt and take a seat by the fire as Lawson picks up trash from dinner. I try to ignore that he didn't mention where Adrian went. I'm sure he's in his cabin with his girlfriend.

"No, don't worry. I've got it." Law's mouth turns up in a smirk, and I laugh, standing up to help him clean up.

"Sorry."

He stops picking up trash, holding the plastic bag in his hand as he looks at me. "Do you know him?"

I'm startled by his question, my eyes darting everywhere but toward him. Eventually, I sigh and meet his gaze. "Who?"

He cocks his head to the side, and yeah, I know that was lame. I know who he's talking about. "Adrian. I saw you go after him. And then, he came back, looking pretty shaken up."

"He left that way. I just thought I should check on him." I take the bag out of his hands. "He's a guest, after all. Isn't it our job to make sure they're comfortable?" I move to the other side of the fire to clean up and get away from his questions, but Law follows me.

"Nash." His voice drips with annoyance—cutting through the bullshit. I like to think I taught him that. "How do you know him?"

"How do you know I know him?" I plop down in one of the chairs, dragging my fingers through my hair.

He chuckles at that and takes the seat next to me. "You're not as stealthy as you think. I've seen you watching him since he walked in. Who is he?"

I can't out Adrian. It's not my place, but I can't really lie to my brother either. "We went to school together." *Not a lie.*

Law's brows furrow. "I don't remember him."

"You were a kid when I graduated."

He huffs and pushes my shoulder. "I'm five years younger than you. I remember most of your class."

I shrug, trying to appear casual. "He moved there his senior year. No reason you should remember him." And we were never seen together. Ever.

"Were you in love with him?"

Again, my brother's words startle me to my core as I look at him in horror. How the hell did he pick up on that? "No." Maybe that's a lie, but maybe it's not. I don't really know what it was with Adrian. We were kids. Kids who never really said how we felt out loud. Who hid in the shadows.

"Nash." He doesn't believe me.

I turn toward the fire, watching the flames flicker in the night. "I don't know what I felt, Law. I was a kid."

"So, he's . . ."

I lock eyes with my brother again and try to convey everything I want to say through my gaze, despite the darkness out here. "No." The word makes me sick, but I push on. "He's with Samantha. He's a senator's son."

Law snorts and rolls his eyes, leaning back in his chair. "A conservative senator's son."

Yeah, he picked up my message. Thank God. I lean back in my own chair and look up at the stars. "An *über*-conservative senator. Yes."

Law looks pissed off as he crosses his arms and gazes up at the stars too. "That's bullshit."

"Don't."

"Don't? Did he hurt you? What did he say?"

I smile, the defensive tone in my brother's voice leaving a warm feeling inside me because he has my back. "He didn't say or do anything. I'm a big boy, Lawson. I can handle it."

He sits up straight, and I feel his eyes on me. "But he did, right? Is he why you don't date? Or why I had no idea you were interested in both guys and girls?"

I swallow thickly, wanting this conversation to be over, but I sigh and sit up, turning toward him. "No. I've always been a loner. You know that. Long before I met Adrian. I'm just . . ." I try to find the words. "I'm better alone."

"That's bullshit."

"It's not." I smile fondly at him. My kid brother—who is no longer a kid.

"It is. You're way too good to be alone forever, Nash. And if his homophobic bullshit did this . . ."

I stop him. "Shhh." I nod toward the cabins, and he bristles but remains quiet. I offer him what I hope is a comforting smile. "Adrian isn't homophobic."

He doesn't look convinced. "Just his family."

It's a statement. "It's all complicated."

"It's not though, right? I mean . . ." He gestures toward Adrian and Samantha's cabin. "He's pretending to be straight for his family's image. It's gross."

A sick feeling fills the pit of my stomach. "You don't know that." He looks like he wants to argue, but I shake my head. "I've been with women, Law. And I wasn't pretending. For all we know, he loves Samantha." The thought makes me bitter, but I try like hell not to show it.

He snorts and shakes his head. "They're plastic. Fake as hell."

"That's just society as a whole, isn't it?" I smile and nudge his arm with mine. "Especially people with a public image."

He shakes his head. "Well, I don't like it. I don't want you hurting, Nash."

"I'm not." I wrap my arm around him and pull him into a side hug. "I'm really not. I'm happier than I've been in a long time. Maybe ever."

*Finally, not a lie.*

He sighs. "Okay. I just don't like it."

I don't either.

"Them being here is good for the cabins." I hit him where it really hurts because I'm an ass. "For Rae."

He stiffens at that and then leans into my hug. "Yeah."

I don't have to say anything else after that.

*We can get through two months with my blast from the past for Rae.*

# Adrian

I COULDN'T SLEEP last night, like barely at all. When I got back from my—whatever the fuck that was— with Nash, I couldn't bear to go into the bedroom with Samantha, so I spent the night tossing and turning on the couch.

I've been haunted by memories of Nash since the day I left him behind, but I've managed to keep them at bay for the most part. But not last night. Last night, I was attacked by every single second I ever spent with him.

The quiet times when we found our way out of the city into our own little world. Deserted roads. The backseat of my car or the back of his truck. Never anywhere anyone could see us.

Occasionally, I got ballsy and took him to my family's lake house. They only used it for parties. So, it was fairly safe. It's where we lost our virginity to each other. It's where I had him inside me for the first time, and where I experienced the bliss of being inside him too.

I toss the throw blanket I had on me to the back of the couch and sit up, digging my palms into my eye sockets and trying to push it all away. I can't think about that time. I can't think about Nash.

It feels like a lifetime ago. When, no matter how miniscule it was, I had hope I could be myself. That I could freely be who I really was. And not just . . .

The thought sours in my gut. Because I can't even think it.

The hope wasn't just that I could be with who I wanted to be with, but that I could stand up for everything I believed. Every misguided concept. Every disgusting policy my family has put in place—not just for our own small familial world but because of their position in national politics, for the entire country and hell, maybe even the world. The most toxic things have a way of branching out.

But I never did it, never stood up for what I believed. Instead, I stayed quiet. I obeyed. I listened and adhered to our legacy and what the Walker name meant. Even if I didn't agree with any of it. Even though I was constantly screaming inside, I went along. And not for any noble reason. Not for any actual threat—not a dire one anyway.

I am now, and have been for most of my life, a coward. I'm not brave. I stay silent. And I'm as guilty as the rest of them. I was conditioned to be this way from birth, and now I'm complacent. I'm numb to it. Walking around like a damn zombie, waiting for them to hand over the kingdom.

I've seen movies and read books where the hero comes in and fiercely—bravely—uses their voice to rescue not only themselves but everyone they love. That's not me. I'm not the person you root for. I'm the antihero.

And I know it.

I drop my hands from my eyes, letting the disgust settle deep inside me, ready to stay there so I can barely function. I look up in time to see Samantha walk out of the bedroom, wearing some sort of slinky, satin red nightie with a matching robe and an eye mask pushed up to sit on top of her head.

She's holding her phone in her hand, but she doesn't look bright and bubbly this morning. She looks almost lost as she walks toward me. "Samantha?" I stand up and move to her. "What's wrong?"

Her eyes meet mine, and she tries to force a smile. "I guess my father isn't coming, at least not this month."

I'm surprised he even bothered telling her. "Yeah. I think he and my father have some business or something to attend to."

She nods her head slowly, and I see her sadness. I feel it because I know that look. We're from the same stock, Samantha and I. Bred solely for excellence but never being good enough for the parents who had such high hopes, no matter what we do. No matter how hard we comply with their demands.

It's sad and a little pathetic because all we really want is their approval. And we'll never get it.

And there it is. I see the instant when she wills away anything real and pushes it aside, leaving in its place a bright, plastic smile. "Well, I guess that's just more time for us to explore. This place is beautiful, isn't it?"

I nod on cue. "It is." Even though I can guess what her answer will be because it's the same one I'd give, I ask, "Are you okay?"

"Yes." Her smile only intensifies as she grabs my hand. "I'm going to shower. Join me."

It's not a question, it's a quiet demand, one I can tell I won't be able to deny, no matter how much it kicks up my heart rate and sends me into a cold sweat.

This shouldn't happen. I shouldn't be close to having a damn panic attack, thinking about being naked with my girlfriend. And yet—that's what happens.

Because it's all a goddamn lie.

She giggles as she pulls me with her. "Relax. I won't tell anyone, Adrian. Your virtue will be protected."

I want to flirt back. Make a joke. Make light of the situation, but I'm just so tired. So very tired of the act. I've managed to keep actual sex off the table until marriage—citing values and a wholesome fucking image. But that doesn't mean Samantha has been satisfied keeping our relationship totally platonic.

When I look at her naked body as she climbs into the steamy glass shower, my body's reaction is that of seeing art at a museum. Something beautiful I can appreciate but not necessarily lust after.

So when I get naked and climb in, soaping up as her hands roam over my body, I blame being tired when my body doesn't react to her soft curves pressing against mine. Samantha is kind enough not to push it, but she has to know.

*Deep down, she has to know something is off.*

That thought has kept me up more nights than I can count. We've traveled a lot, usually staying in separate hotel rooms and the fact that we're staying in the same cabin on this trip must attest to her father's plans to cement the whole deal.

He wants this marriage, I think, even more than my father. Wants me to help break Samantha, bend her to his will. And God help me, I'm sure I will. Although, not forcefully like her father would. But it will happen over years and years of our silent, loveless marriage. To end things with her would take an actual hero.

To admit that what we have isn't real. To tell my father I want nothing to do with politics.

*All of it takes a far stronger man than I'll ever be.*

# Nash

"RAE, IT'S FINE." I try to calm her down as she flies around the dining hall, trying to fix the place settings that look the same to me as they did ten minutes ago.

She shoots me an exasperated look. "Nash. Did you see the way they looked at the hotdogs last night? We need to step up our game."

Lawson takes her small shoulders in his hands, effectively calming her, and making her stay in one spot for a second. "Our goal is to be different, remember? Memorable. We did the bonfire with the traditional campfire food. And Samantha loved it."

Rae plops down in a vacant seat and seems to relax. At least for Rae. "I know. I mean according to her Insta stories, she thought the food was charming."

Charming? What the fuck? Food can be charming?

I think my face must say what I was thinking because my sister in law looks irritated again. "What?"

"What?" I raise my hands in surrender. "Charming. That's good. Right?"

She huffs, her eyes widening comically as she stares me down. "Right."

I offer a smile. It's forced, and she knows it. "Good."

That, for whatever it is, makes her giggle and toss a cloth napkin at me. "You are such a bad liar."

"All I said was 'good,'" I laugh. The girl pulls it out of me. What can

I say?

Lawson takes a seat next to her and across from me. "It is good. The website nearly crashed last night from bookings."

"No shit?" I ask, pleasantly surprised.

Lawson is practically beaming now. "Yeah. We're already booked until May.

*Holy shit.* I knew Samantha had some influence, but damn. Makes it hard to hate her. I mean . . . I don't. Of course, I don't. She hasn't done anything to me.

The doors to the dining hall open hesitantly as a woman pokes her head inside, and Rae pops up to greet them. She, her husband, and five young kids checked in last night, and they now flood into the room.

Tammy and Hayden direct them to the breakfast buffet that they and Rae were up early this morning preparing. I'm more the manual labor around here. They don't dare let me near the stove.

And before I know it, all the occupants of the cabins are under the roof, including Adrian and his über-smiley fiancé. When everyone has helped themselves, Rae and Law sit down with Samantha and Adrian. I'm also instructed to sit down by Hayden, who plops a full plate in front of me and takes a seat across from Adrian.

My seat is facing Adrian's soon-to-be fiancé head-on, but thankfully Rae is right at her side and keeping her busy with idle small talk.

Samantha is busy gushing about her bonfire posts from the night before while I stare at the stack of French toast on my plate and try like hell to ignore Adrian. I can smell his cologne from where I sit and sense his gaze like a beacon from hell's past.

"So when do your parents arrive?" Rae asks, and I hesitantly look up, sensing Adrian's body going stiff at the question.

Samantha however keeps her previous smile plastered to her pretty face, waving her hand as if pushing away anything bad. "Oh. Well, my mother should be here in a couple of hours. But it seems, my father won't be here for a couple of weeks."

My eyes catch Adrian's no matter how much I try to resist, and I see the ire in them. My right eyebrow arches in a silent question, but his pink lips are pursed shut while his eyes remain cold and refuse to give anything away. But I can feel the tension.

"Oh, I'm sorry about your father. But I can't wait to meet your mother." Rae bounces back from the semi-awkward moment.

Samantha's smile only widens, but it doesn't seem real to me. "Yeah. She's great."

"She'll be taking the final cabin?"

Samantha nods her head in an answer, pulling out her phone. "Yes. And eventually my father will join her." She starts to scan the room with her camera. "I just have to document this wonderful breakfast."

Rae smiles when the camera lands on her, and Samantha talks as if addressing a large crowd. I lean over to talk to Hayden quietly. "What the fuck is she doing?"

Hayden laughs at me, his mouth moving to my ear in an answer. "Going live. We really need to get you an Instagram."

I shake my head at that and grimace. "No, thanks."

He shoves me playfully. "Okay, gramps."

I roll my eyes at him and laugh until my eyes meet Adrian's again, which have gone from impassive to full-on furious. The fire burning in those hazels nearly makes my heart stop for a moment, the intensity of the past bubbling up to the surface in an instant.

Samantha aims her phone in my direction, and I immediately straighten up and away from Hayden, mindful of Adrian's warning from the night before, and I cringe instantly. *Goddammit, how is it the same man has me hiding years later?*

I want to raise my middle finger to everyone in that video that might have a problem with Hayden and me being together. But instead, I stand there stiffly and grab my coffee mug, taking a drink as I wait for her to move away from me.

Luckily, I'm a boring subject, and she moves on pretty fast. When she puts the phone down, she takes the world's smallest bite of French toast and moans dramatically in Adrian's direction. "Oh my God, that is absolutely delicious." She cuts another piece and holds the fork in front of Adrian's lips—lips I've kissed, lips I've been obsessed with. He opens for her, taking a bite.

He chews silently, his body rigid, and then I'm sure to most, it looks like a smile forms on his lips, but to me, it looks more like a grimace. "Very good."

It takes everything in me not to scoff. *Why is he faking everything? No. You don't care.*

But it's so damn obvious as she touches his arm, and he looks like he nearly recoils, like he can't stand her touch. But then, he smiles at her and covers her hand with his. My mind is at war with itself as I watch their exchange. It's all very polite. *Clinical.*

"Hey, are you going to eat at all?" I pry my eyes off Adrian and see Samantha turning to Hayden, who's watching me closely.

"What?"

He chuckles and nods to his plate. "*Eat.* We have quite a morning, and you're going to need your energy, big guy."

I feel Adrian's heated gaze on me now, and my lips turn up in a sweet smile that's aimed at Hayden but is all for Adrian's benefit. "Ah, that's right. We're going to work all of it off this morning."

Hayden is talking about cutting firewood, but it doesn't sound like it. And I played it up. *Why? I have no fucking clue.*

I just wink at Hayden and dig into my breakfast. When I see Adrian watching me with anger boiling in his gaze, I smirk in his direction.

Hating that I'm playing games.

Hating that I can't seem to stop myself.

But still participating in it because everything is there at the forefront of my mind. Him promising me he'd be there at his parent's lake house. Me believing him like an idiot. Him never showing and my heart cracking in two as the sun rose over the horizon. And now, watching him with a woman I'm sure was handpicked by his family.

The woman he's going to share the rest of his life with because of some sort of twisted obligation he's always felt to his family.

I've watched them. Maybe only for twenty-four hours, but one thing is for certain to me, deep down.

*He doesn't love her.*

My axe smashes through the large piece of wood, splintering it in two and falling to the earth below before I pick up another piece and repeat the process. It's cold out here this morning, but sweat is soaking through my shirt and my coat as I split the firewood repeatedly, taking out all my aggression from breakfast.

He doesn't love her. I know he doesn't because I've seen passion from Adrian. I've seen fiery lust burning in his eyes. I've seen desire and his need to tear clothes from his lover's body. Dying to be alone.

I've seen it, and that was not it.

"Whoa." Hayden stares at me, looking a little frightened but also amused. "Easy there, tiger." He picks up another piece of wood and puts it on the stump, but he doesn't move, even though I'm holding an axe. "You want to talk about it?"

"No." I gesture for him to move, but he doesn't. He just cocks his perfectly groomed eyebrow at me and waits. "Hayden . . ."

"Come on, Nash. We're best friends. Even though I would love to get a little closer. You know, all naked and sweaty, although, you seem hellbent on that not happening." He winks at me. "Still, we're close."

"You're something else."

He laughs at that, his light, beautiful laugh extremely contagious. "Yeah. So I've been told. But what was that at breakfast?"

"I have no idea what you're talking about."

He rolls his eyes dramatically at me. "Yes. You do. That whole appetite thing. I mean, don't get me wrong. I liked the inuendo. I'm going to use it later."

"Hayden." My voice has a pleading lilt to it because I don't want to talk about this.

"It's him, right?" He takes a step back from the stump, but he doesn't drop it. "The senator's son. The beautiful, well-groomed blond man you haven't been able to stop staring at. He's the one guy."

The rest of his sentence wasn't a question because he knows the answer. When the hell did I become so damn transparent?

"Hayden." I manage to make my voice sound a little stronger. But it doesn't deter him.

"Damn, what are the odds? Of all the places in the world, the one guy you've been with walks into our humble cabins. That's fate." His eyes are wide with wonder now, and I avoid it by bringing my axe down, splintering the wood into two pieces.

"Adrian Walker is staying here with his girlfriend. He's a guest."

Hayden picks up another piece of wood and places it for me. "But that's not all he is."

"I can't . . ." I don't finish my sentence and tell him that I can't out Adrian. Because I can't. And Hayden knows that, so I don't even have to really tell him. It's not my place to out him or anyone else.

"I know. But this must be impossible for you."

I feel the weight of that before letting the blade of my axe release some of the tension, taking it out on the firewood again. "It's fine."

"It's not. What happened between you and that boy?" He offers the question with enough vagueness that I feel like I can answer. Almost. And Hayden must pick up on it because he adds, "The boy from your past? The one guy you were with before you decided to live a dick-free life."

I roll my eyes at him but smirk. "I have a dick. My life will never be dick-free."

"Wanna prove it?" He waggles his eyebrows, and I shake my head. "You're ridiculous."

"Talk to me. You can't hold it all in, Nash. That shit will kill you."

I continue my work, and he assists. But I know he's right, and eventually I huff and start talking about that boy. Not Adrian. "Nothing really happened. We were kids. Neither of us had been with a guy before. Or really anyone. I had kissed a few girls, but I had done some time in juvie . . ."

"Yeah. Lawson told me about that. You stole to keep the lights on for your family. You aren't going to convince me you're the bad guy."

I snort and shake my head again. My mom had a hard time supporting us, having an on and off again relationship with drugs, and I got busted for shoplifting. But I went to juvie because I was already on thin ice and got into a fight, breaking the other guy's nose. I was an angry kid. "I'm not the good guy either."

He waves me off. "Continue. Get to the good stuff."

I laugh, and then we switch, I gather the wood while he splits it with the axe. "We snuck around. All the time. We never did anything in public, barely even looked at each other. It wasn't just him that wanted it that way, but after awhile . . ." I sigh, and Hayden meets my eyes with a knowing look. "I wanted more. I wanted him."

"And he wasn't ready to come out."

"I don't think that boy will ever be ready."

He nods his head, looking back toward the cabins and then toward me. "I'm assuming this boy's family wasn't supportive. And are all-around douchebags."

"Understatement."

His nose crinkles. "So what happened?"

"I told him I loved him." My heart speeds up in my chest, thinking about that night, lying spent and totally naked with him tucked to my side when I whispered the words. He whispered them back, and then we went for round two.

"And?" Hayden is getting impatient, and it makes me laugh, despite the painful memories.

"We made a plan. We'd graduated from high school, and he was supposed to be going to college, but we wanted to be together. At least, that's what we told each other." The bitterness seeps through my words. "I was an idiot, Hayden. I believed him. That we were going to make our own way. We were eighteen. We were going to pack our bags and leave. Hop on a train and go wherever we wanted. Find jobs and live that life together."

His expression has saddened as he listens.

"But the night he was supposed to meet me at his parent's lake house, I waited all night, and he never showed. He didn't call. Nothing. And the next day, I used a friend's Facebook account and saw a post he was tagged in about him leaving for college."

"He just left?"

I nod. The memory heavy on my soul. I cried for the first time I can remember. Alone in my bedroom, staring at the beige wall. I sobbed for hours, begging for an explanation.

"Yes."

"Jesus, Nash."

"It doesn't matter now. I'm over it."

"Except that you aren't. I mean . . . Come on. I've seen you watching him. The intensity. The bitterness. That's totally warranted."

I can't mesh the two people together, so I say, "I don't know anything about that boy from back then. Nothing. And I'm happy in my life now."

He scoffs at that before splitting the firewood again and pinning me with a look. "You don't date. As far as I know, you've been a monk for the couple of years I've known you."

"Not everyone has to have a lot of sex to be happy, Hayden."

"That does not compute, but I suppose you're right. Still. I think you do, but you're scared. Maybe you need to confront your past."

"No, thanks."

We switch again, and I take over the axe because frankly I'm tense and need some stress relief. He lets me and finally drops it.

I can't think about that boy from the past and the fact that he's a mere hundred steps away from me.

*I can't think about him at all.*

# Adrian

A FEW DAYS have passed now without incident, and I'm grateful for the small victory. I nearly lost my shit at breakfast the other day, watching Nash and Hayden right before my eyes, talking about getting all hot and sweaty together.

Hayden is beautiful. I can't blame Nash, but goddammit, I warned him. Thankfully, Samantha didn't seem to pick up on their relationship at all. I'm finishing up a couple of business emails when she walks into the bedroom, her eyes zoning in on the phone in my hand.

"What are you doing?" She cocks her head to the side in question.

"Just working a little bit. You know this world never stops."

I see a flash of what I think is anger on her face as she approaches me. "You're working? Here?"

I put my phone down, eyeing her cautiously. "Just for a moment." *Is she actually pissed? Is she going to let me see it?*

"Oh." And then, whatever I thought I saw disappears into thin air. She forces a smile and waves it off. "Well, are you finished? Because there's a hot tub outside I really want to try out."

I don't know what makes me push, but I'm so damn tired of the act. I sit up a little straighter on the bed, narrowing my eyes. "You can tell me, you know." She cocks her head to the side slightly, and I continue, "If it upsets you that I'm working."

Again, her small, manicured hand waves it all away. "Of course, it

63

doesn't upset me. You're an ambitious man. It's one of the many things that attracted me to you," she purrs as she comes closer to the bed.

I'm really not ambitious at all. My biggest dream is to disappear into the world, never to be seen or brought up again. Not even to explore the horizon—just to be left alone. To be me. Never to see my face on the television screen, dressed in a stiff suit as they predict when I'll pop the question.

"I'm not your father."

Again, I think I might see an actual emotion. Good. I want to see it. I want her to yell at me, to scream at me. I want to feel something, goddammit. Anything. Her eyes darken, and I prepare myself for any of that. But then she sits down on the edge of the bed with her back perfectly straight and laughs, but it's calculated. Perfect. "Of course, you aren't, sweetie. But you have obligations. I know you can't get away for the entire two months."

I stare at her, trying like hell to see anything real in her. "But you could ask me to," I prod. "I mean, you asked us all to do that, remember? And my dad left after one day. Your dad never showed." I wait, studying her perfectly poised features that don't flinch. "You can be upset that I'm working too."

She stands up and sighs softly, crossing her arms as she looks down at me. "What are you doing?"

"I'm not doing anything." I stand up and walk over to her. "But . . . Samantha." I graze her cheek with my hand. "Don't you ever get sick of it? Everyone letting you down?"

Briefly—ever so briefly—she looks almost sad, like she might agree. But then, she covers my hand with hers and shakes her head. "I'm surrounded by powerful men. It makes me proud."

I sigh and drop my hand, frustrated that she won't show me even a hint of earnest emotion. That we're both so broken and everything is so practiced, that *this* is our normal existence.

I stare at her, unsure of what to say. But then, a loud sound rings out from the woods behind the cabin, startling us both. "What is that?"

Samantha looks so horrified, I would probably laugh if I wasn't a robot.

"I think it's a chainsaw."

Her button nose crinkles. "Oh no. That's way too loud, and I'm scheduled to go live in thirty minutes."

"I thought you wanted to check out the hot tub?" I question.

Her bottom lip pokes out. "After I go live." Her voice takes on a little more of a whine now. "Can you please go tell them to keep it down? I need to prepare."

I don't bother arguing because while she doesn't show disappointment in her father, mother, or me, she sure as fuck won't stand for letting her followers down with a little background noise.

I grab my coat and go out the front door in search of the loud sound. And then I find it. In the form of Nash Fucking Davis. He's wearing only a red and black flannel shirt and jeans with a chainsaw in his hand, lost to the world as he cuts down a tree.

It's cold as hell out here, but he doesn't seem to notice as he works. Chopping the tree to pieces and no doubt driving my girlfriend to a near meltdown. "Nash!" I holler over the loud motor. He doesn't stop what he's doing, so I'm louder as I get closer. "Nash!"

He falters, straightening up and turning the chainsaw off to glare at me. "What are you doing out here?"

I motion toward the chainsaw in his hand. "It's pretty loud."

He scoffs. "Did I interrupt your beauty sleep? It's only eight o'clock."

"No. My girlfriend needs quiet though, she's trying to work." I straighten my shoulders, trying to assert my authority.

"Girlfriend," he scoffs, and it instantly pisses me off as I take another step in his direction.

"What the fuck does that mean? How is that funny?"

He puts the chainsaw down and takes off his leather gloves I only now notice he was wearing, taking a step in my direction. "It's funny because you have zero attraction to her, and yet, you're calling her your girlfriend and are ready to propose to her."

I stop my gasp at his accusation, but just barely. "What?"

He shakes his head, tossing the gloves onto the ground next to the chainsaw and coming closer to me. "You heard me."

"You don't know what the hell you're talking about. Samantha is a beautiful woman. Of course, I'm attracted to her."

Nash only shakes his head from side to side again, pursing his full lips in thought. "That she is, but you aren't attracted to her. You don't love her. And the fact that you're still faking it . . ."

"Fuck you." I meet him, the toes of my dress shoes touching the tip of his boots.

"Hit a nerve?"

"No," I snarl, "You're just wrong. I'm in love with her. I'm not faking anything."

"You flinch every time she touches you."

My eyes widen, and my heart skips a quick beat before starting to race. "That's not true."

"It is. It's like you can't bear her touch. And yet, you keep going. Why, Adrian?"

I feel dizzy and take a step back, but he only takes one forward. "I don't know what you think you saw, but you're wrong."

"Yeah?"

I nod my head and step back again, retreating, but he follows. "Yes."

"So, when she touches you, you don't recoil?" I swallow hard and shake my head as my back comes into contact with a hard tree. "You feel nothing but desire?" His voice is a husky whisper, his breath smells of fresh mint, like maybe he's been sucking on a peppermint as he works.

He used to taste like mint.

I try to push that thought away, but his close contact along with his words is making everything so damn fuzzy. "I d-do, desire her."

"Right." He doesn't believe me. He just cocks his head to the side and studies me as my desperate breaths push my chest against his with each puff, the cold air not helping the intensity of the situation. "So, when she kisses you, you feel like you've been set on fire? Like you're desperate to be owned by her, to possess her?" I watch his lips move in the dark night only lit by the moon and stars above. "When she touches you, it's like you can't catch your breath because you need her that badly?"

I suck in a startled breath, my chest feeling like it's on fire from sucking in the cold air. "Y-yes."

"Liar."

That sends rage through me, and my hand presses against his hard chest. I think it was to push him away, but it just stays there like a fucking traitor. "I'm not a liar."

"No?" He laughs humorlessly. "Should we go over all the things you've lied about?"

"No," I say entirely too quickly.

His eyes move to where my hand is still resting on the soft flannel of the shirt covering his chest. "No? Then admit it. Admit that you aren't attracted to her."

I lick my lips, the cold air hitting them. "I . . .

"You what?" he prods, pushing my buttons, pissing me off, and challenging me like he always has.

This version is darker than the sweet boy I once knew. But still challenging. I close my eyes, and I hear his voice telling me I deserve better. That I shouldn't have to hide any part of myself.

I open my eyes and glare deep into his. "I'm marrying her. She's beautiful and smart. Of course, I'm attracted to her."

His jaw is clenched, his frustration pouring off him, but he doesn't back down. He doesn't put on a façade for me. "Why are you doing this? To please daddy, all these years later?"

"You know nothing about me, Nash. Nothing."

"You're right." His words sting. It's two simple words, and they cut me deep. "I don't know you. Because the boy I thought I knew, he was good. He had a fucking soul, even if he was scared. But marrying someone solely to please your father when you aren't in love with them . . ." He shakes his head in sheer disappointment. "That's low. And that's nothing like the boy I knew."

"You didn't know him either, Nash. You saw . . ." My breath is visible in the cold as I pause for a moment, my eyes closing again with the memories of him. "You thought I was good. Far better than I was."

My eyes open, and he's watching me. His face is so damn close to me. "Yeah. Maybe."

*Hate me.*

My eyes plead with him. "I'm not good. I don't want to be."

"So you're going to marry her then." It's not a question.

I drop my hand, but he surprises me by putting his hand on my chest. My coat is open, and his big hand lands over my beating heart that only starts pounding harder and faster at the contact. "Yes."

We stand like that for way too long. His hand over my heart, our breath mingling in the cold night air, standing mere inches from each other.

I feel more alive now than I have in years, and when he leans in closer, I want his lips on mine. My entire body is pleading for it. When he bypasses my mouth, and his lips nearly touch my ear, I think I stop breathing for a moment. "Go."

*What?*

I stand frozen, and then when he steps back, taking his hand off my chest, leaving behind a cold, numb feeling, I open my mouth to say the words. To beg him to come back. To not leave me. To tell him I know I'm a coward, but I want to be better.

*But I don't.*

I don't say a damn thing.

I simply let him go back to work as I silently walk away.

*Like I always do.*

*I TOUCHED HIM.*

*I fucking touched him.*

*What the hell is wrong with me?*

It was a brief contact, but I felt his rapid heartbeat under my palm, and I looked into his eyes, seeing the pleading there.

After all these years. He still wants me. I could feel it.

But I couldn't go there. Not again. I can't go back to hiding who I am. If he wants to live that way, it's his choice. But I can't do it.

I'm drained from the short interaction, and instead of continuing to cut down trees for firewood, I go in search of someone who will ground me.

I find Lawson in his small studio we built over the summer. Like I said, he's one of the most talented artists I've ever seen. And while he didn't get his chance in art school, he's perfected his craft over the years.

Selling to the tourists who come here as well as to the locals. He's also designed a website now that he's started to gain a following. He's busy working on a beautiful, vibrant piece when I walk through the door and doesn't even notice me. So lost in his own world.

I clear my throat, and he startles for a second before he sees it's me. "Hey, you done making all that noise?"

I roll my eyes and take a seat on one of the stools near him. "It's not that loud."

Although, I know it was irritating everyone tonight. He laughs at that, dragging his brush over the canvas. "It was, but we need the firewood. So thank you."

"You're welcome." I nod toward the painting. "Almost ready?"

He stands back for a moment, studying his work and shakes his head. "Not quite." He puts the brush down and then takes a seat on the stool next to me. "Samantha wants to do a post about my art." He sounds hesitant.

"That's a good thing, right?"

"Yeah." His eyes light up. "But." And then they dim, and I see the self-doubt there I don't like at all.

"Lawson . . ."

"Nash," he shoots back, and I smile.

"It will be great. Her posting about this place has us booked for months. Imagine what she can do for your art."

It leaves a bitter taste in my mouth, but I know it's true. There's no denying her insane influence, and the fact that she's doing it for free is incredible. "I know." But he doesn't sound convinced, so I wait. His eyes meet mine, and for a second, I see my kid brother, vulnerable and afraid. "It feels like I'm selling out."

I smile fondly. "Always the artist."

"Fuck you." He says it with a smile.

Which only makes me laugh. "Lawson." I hold his gaze. "Your art should be seen by the world. Even when you were really little, I knew that you were special. Let her help you."

He seems to let that soak in. "What if I fuck up the brand?"

I laugh at that, not cruelly, but genuinely surprised he could ever think that. I look back at the bold colors on the canvas and smile. "Not gonna happen. It will only help the cabins' popularity. You'll see."

He stands up, looks at his painting and then back at me as I rise from my seat. "Okay. I'll man up and let her see it." I pat his shoulder with my hand, and he grins. "Let's go."

"Where?"

"Hot tub and margarita party." I groan, and he only laughs, leading me toward the door. "It was Hayden's idea, and Samantha was all over it. She wants to show her followers how fun it is here."

"Of course, this was Hayden's idea."

"Yup. Let's go."

He locks up his studio, and I huff, trying to think of a way out of this. The last thing I want is to be in a hot tub with Adrian and his soon-to-be fiancé. "I'm sweaty and gross. I can't get in the hot tub."

"So go take a shower."

"That's stupid. If I shower, then why would I get into the hot tub?"

He gives me an irritated look that makes him look younger again. "Because your brother asked you to. And it will be fun."

"Fun," I scoff, but I sigh, knowing I'm not getting out of this. "Fine."

He grins, knowing he's getting his way and heads off toward the hot tub area behind the dining hall. I head into my cabin and strip, wondering what the chances are of Hayden dragging my ass to the party if I don't show up.

Deciding they're pretty high, I hop into the shower and under the hot water, reveling in the warmth. It's a stark contrast from the cold outside. The water sluicing over my body feels good on my sore muscles as I stand under the spray, unmoving.

I can't believe I touched him. I let him touch me. I close my eyes and place my hand on the marble of the shower wall. He smelled good. So damn good. I couldn't stop staring at his lips, even though they were snarling and moving fast with his angry rant.

He's a fucking liar.

I try to remind myself, even as I drag in breath after breath, and think about how badly I wanted to feel more of him. How desperately I wanted to kiss him again. To see if his lips were just as soft and pliant as they once were.

Without my permission, my cock starts to harden with the thoughts of him. I try to ignore it. I don't want to want him.

I grab my soap and quickly wash my body, trying to be quick when I move over my dick. But my hand strokes slowly instead, enjoying the grip and the slippery suds, allowing my hand to glide effortlessly over my aching erection.

*I don't want him.*

*I don't.*

A soft whimper escapes me when I think about his hand on me through my shirt, and I nearly lose it after a few slow strokes, but I stop myself. I yank my hand away and turn the water to a cooler temperature.

I won't give into him, even if he's not here. I won't do it.

I climb out of the shower, willing my dick to go down, and it only half obliges before I tug on a pair of red swim trunks.

It's fucking freezing outside. Hayden is nuts.

I pull on my coat over my trunks, not bothering with anything else other than my boots and head out into the blistery cold hell, making my way out to the hot tubs. We have two, but only one seems to be on at the moment.

There's loud music as Hayden prances around in a white fluffy robe and slippers, filling up glasses with margaritas and singing to the music I'm sure he picked. He sees me and immediately laughs, covering his mouth and shaking his head. "You know, we have robes."

I hear Rae and Tammy's giggles from the hot tub and look at my sister-in-law. "What?"

She looks down at my boots. "Only you would wear full winter boots to a hot tub party."

"It's cold," I say and look over at Hayden as he hands me a glass. "And Hayden didn't give me any fuzzy slippers."

I take the margarita from Hayden as he winks at me. "That's going on your Christmas list, sweetie."

*No. Doubt.* I grumble and place the glass on the outdoor bar, before kicking my boots off. "Happy?"

Lawson, who's next to Rae in the hot tub, whistles. "I see your ankles! Cover your eyes, girls!"

"I'm going to drown you."

I hear another laugh I'm not as used to, and my eyes shift to Samantha, who's wearing a purple bikini top and leaning against Adrian, who's wearing a grim expression as he glares at me. His bare chest is smooth except for a light dusting of golden hair, and he's more toned than he was last time I saw him shirtless but not overly so. His face is painfully beautiful even through his rage, maybe even more so because of it.

He's still staring daggers at me, no doubt still worked-up from our earlier conversation. Pissed off that I called him on his bullshit.

*He's angry.*

*Good.*

*Feeling is mutual, asshole.*

# Adrian

HE LOOKS RIDICULOUS. Even after he slips out of his boots. He's wearing bright red swim trunks that go to his knees and a heavy winter coat. I'll admit when Samantha and I arrived at the back deck where two hot tubs are located, I was relieved to not see Nash.

And I thought we'd get through the night without his presence, but I was wrong because here he is. And he looks about as happy as I do about it.

His friends continue to rib him about his attire, but then Hayden finishes pouring drinks and joins us in the hot tub, and the conversation picks up again. All moving on except for me.

Because my eyes are glued to the surly, unfairly sexy bearded man outside of the hot tub. He unzips the heavy coat and places it on a chair outside, but my mouth instantly waters at the sight.

*Jesus.*

I knew he had bulked up since the last time I saw him, his shirts begging for mercy and busting at the seams, trying to contain his muscular arms. But seeing his ripped abs, it's apparent the muscles don't stop with the arms.

He's cut from absolute stone, and he's added some tattoos on his upper arms and his back. He's toned perfection all the way down to a stupid V pointing right down to a beautifully long, thick cock, hidden beneath the trunks.

*Shit. Thank God I'm in the water. How long have I been staring?*

I focus on Samantha, my beautiful girlfriend who's having fun talking to Tammy, Rae, Hayden, and Lawson while I'm busy drooling over a man.

Nash joins us, sitting right next to Hayden. Of course, he is. Leave it to his stubborn ass not to heed my warning. I don't think Samantha would say anything if she saw they were a couple. But dammit, why risk it?

Samantha pulls her phone out, telling everyone she's going live and getting a verbal okay for them to be in it. They all agree, and she pans the camera around, telling her followers how much fun she's having here.

When she zones in on Nash's ripped bod, I see involuntary red, thinking about all the viewers who'll be drooling over him. "The staff here is not only beautiful, but insanely friendly and fun, you guys!" Samantha speaks to them through her video, and I know it will be a hit. People will flock here, and it warms my insides, thinking about that.

When I knew Nash before, he cared so much for his little brother. He only wanted him happy, and now his business is flourishing. It doesn't make up for what I did to him—not that I really had anything to do with it—but still it helps a little to know Samantha's presence is helping Nash and his family.

After the live stream, we all seem to relax and just enjoy the margaritas and relaxing hot water. All except for Hayden, who I notice is watching me closely. And he doesn't seem as happy as he did before. *Did Nash tell him about us? Does he think I'm a threat?*

It's ridiculous, but the guy is usually all smiles. Something seems off. When it starts to get late, Lawson and Raelynn excuse themselves. Then Samantha turns to me, wrapping her arm around my shoulders. "Are you ready to go to bed? I'm beat."

*I should go.* For sure, I should go, but I have too many questions. "You go ahead. I think I'll stay for a bit."

She looks surprised, but of course, she doesn't fight me. She just climbs out of the hot tub and pulls on her robe before leaving me alone with the happy couple and Tammy, who doesn't stay long before bouncing off to her cabin.

It's an awkward silence while I wait a reasonable amount of time but then narrow my eyes at Nash. "Did you tell him about us?"

"Us?" Nash raises a cocky eyebrow, and I glare.

"Yes," I hiss and then look in the direction of Hayden, who definitely has his hackles raised. "Your boyfriend has been giving me the stink eye all night."

"Boyfriend?" Hayden seems amused but angry at the same time.

"He's not my boyfriend," Nash supplies, and I look at him, studying him closely.

"But you . . ."

He shakes his head at me, his jaw clenched tight. "You assumed."

I think back to our conversations, and while he never denied it, I guess he never confirmed they were together either. "Well, whatever you two are, you aren't exactly being discreet."

"Discreet?" Hayden says, clearly offended, and I flinch only slightly. I know it's fucked up.

Before I can explain anything, Nash interjects angrily, "I would never ask him to hide who he is. Not for me or for anyone else. Ever. That's fucked up."

It is. Bile rises in my throat, just thinking about the words I've said. Words coming from my father indirectly through me. I hate it, but I straighten my shoulders. "Not even for the good of your brother's cabins?"

Hayden rolls his eyes and shakes his head at me. "I'm too gay for *you?*"

The way he says it sends a shiver down my spine, his eyes boring through me like he knows everything about me. I turn to Nash. "You did tell him."

"He didn't tell me anything about you." Hayden is defensive. And protective over Nash in a way that both makes me jealous—because I wanted to be that man for him—and happy because he has someone in his corner. Someone who isn't a goddamn coward. "He told me about a boy. A boy so scared of who he was that he let an amazing man like Nash go."

I swallow hard, hating that there are actual tears forming in my eyes that I refuse to let fall. I look at Hayden. "That boy is a man now."

"Is he?"

I want to argue, but I know he's right. I'm just a scared little boy trapped in a man's body. "Look." I try to gain composure, channel my asshole father, and remain businesslike. "I don't care that you're gay. I don't care that you're fucking Nash." *Lie.* "But my soon-to-be in-laws and my father, they will destroy this place if you aren't discreet about it. I want this place to do well."

"You're unbelievable." Hayden is pissed and stands up, showing off his reindeer covered small swim trunks. "Just because you deny who you are doesn't mean we're all stuck in the closet."

I turn to Nash, unsure why I think he'll back me up. "This place is packed because of Samantha."

"Samantha seems to like Hayden just fine." I know she does.

"She's not the problem." Hayden climbs out, putting on his robe and his fuzzy slippers.

"Hayden, I didn't mean anything by it. I'm happy for you and Nash."

"We aren't together." Nash says it again. "We're friends. But I still won't ever ask him to be anything other than who he is. That's cruel."

"The cruelest. And thanks." Hayden winks at him before turning to me. "I feel sorry for you. It's not easy hiding who you really are, and I'll never out anyone no matter what. Your secret is safe with me."

That should make me feel relief, but all I feel is overwhelming guilt. "I'm sorry." I croak out the words but just barely.

He offers me a sad smile and then blows Nash a kiss before leaving. I stay immersed in the water, across from Nash where we just glare at each other.

Finally, he speaks. "They guessed."

"They?" I ask, horrified.

"My brother and Hayden. I'd just told them about a guy I was with right before you got here. I didn't tell them who you were, but they guessed."

I swallow thickly. "How?"

He laughs humorlessly, "I guess it was obvious to them. I don't know. But you don't have to worry. They have more integrity than anyone you know now or will ever know."

I don't doubt it. "Okay."

"That's all?"

"What else is there to say? I can't help you if you won't help yourself."

He snorts and stands up, showing off all that insane skin wrapping around his hard muscles. "Help myself? By making Hayden what? Tone down his offensive *gayness*?"

"I didn't say it was offensive."

"But it is, right? To them." He nods toward the cabins and then pins me with an enraged look. "It somehow offends their *wholesome* lifestyle, true?"

I stand up too, exiting the hot tub when Nash does. It's fucking cold now, but neither of us try to dry off or cover up. We just stand there. "I can't speak for them."

"But you do. You speak for them every day when you choose to hide who you really are. You carry out their sick agenda."

I stare at him, shivering from the cold and his words. Goosebumps cover my flesh. "What do you want from me, Nash?"

"Absolutely nothing."

I stare into his dark eyes and breathe in the cold air.

"Men like Hayden disgust them," He leans in, his lips grazing my ear and making me shiver for a whole new reason. "They would absolutely lose it if they knew the things I've done to you." I suck in a harsh breath. "The things you did to me."

I close my eyes, thinking about the moments of passion between us. The kissing. The touching. Him inside me. Me inside him. His mouth. God, his mouth was magical. "Nash." I don't know if it's a plea for him to stop or to keep going, and it scares the hell out of me. "I can't do this."

"There's nothing to do." He pulls back, his eyes meeting mine. "But don't ask me to hide who I am. I'm never doing that again."

This time, he leaves. Hastily pulling on his coat and his boots and walking away. I stand there for far too long, letting the cold, blistery air batter my skin.

*I deserve far worse.*

*Adrian*

I MAKE it back to the cabin, freezing my ass off, wearing the fluffy white robe and slippers provided for the cabin guests. But I'm numb from more than the cold. I can't get past the look of pity in Hayden's eyes and the fire in Nash's.

God, I admire the hell out of both men. They know who they are, and they hold their heads high. I want that. Desperately. But I've never let myself admit it until now.

Samantha is sitting in a chair by the fireplace, wrapped up in a blanket with a glass of wine next to her and her phone in her hand. She looks up at me and smiles sweetly. "Hey, I was about to come check on you."

I doubt that. We don't really check up on each other. "Yeah?" I plop down on the couch, and she looks over at me, studying me closely.

Her small shoulders shrug. "Well, I thought maybe you were having fun though. I didn't want to interrupt."

The way she says it has me on full alert. *Did she overhear something? No. She was long gone before we started our discussion.* "No. There wouldn't have been anything to interrupt. Just hanging out with the staff."

*God, I sound like a snob.*

"Right." She's smiling again, but it's like she knows a secret.

"Right. What's up?"

81

She giggles now. Placing her phone on her lap. "Adrian, it's fine. I saw how you were looking at Tammy. She's beautiful."

*Wait. What?* I stare at her dumbfounded. "Tammy?"

"Yeah. Tammy. She's flirtatious and funny too. I don't blame you for wanting to spend a little extra time with her." She waggles her eyebrows, and I stare at her in horror, trying to figure out what the hell is going on. She thinks I'm interested in Tammy, and is she implying that I cheated on her?

"Nothing happened with Tammy."

She waves me off and takes a drink of wine. "I don't need details, Adrian."

I sit up straighter and look directly at her, "I would never cheat on you. Ever. I'm not a cheater."

She nearly chokes on her wine and recovers, placing the glass down as she laughs. "Of course, you aren't. It's not cheating."

"What are you implying then? Because nothing happened."

Again, she waves me off, looking so unbothered I want to scream. "Okay, okay. I believe you. But you know you can do something if you want to."

"What?"

She cocks her head to the side and huffs at me like I'm the one who's gone crazy. "Adrian, I'm not under the insanely naïve impression that you have never touched anyone else."

"Before us . . ."

She laughs. "Come on. I'm not doing this, okay? I'm not my mother."

"What's that supposed to mean?" I'm trying to navigate this conversation, but I'm so totally lost.

She sighs and leans forward slightly, talking slow as if that's why I'm having trouble here. "I'm not going to sit at home and convince myself that you're being totally faithful to me. I'm just not. We don't have to do that. I trust you to be discreet and safe. That's really all I care about."

My jaw drops. She thinks I'm fucking around on her. And more than that, she's fine with it. "Samantha, I'm not your father or mine. I'm faithful. I haven't touched anyone since we got together."

It's the truth. I'm many things, but I'm not a cheater.

She leans back in her chair and shakes her head. "It's fine, Adrian. Really. Go and have as much fun as you want. Wear a rubber. It's not like I'm sitting around pining after you, and we have a great relationship."

I stand up now, shocked to my core. "What the fuck does that mean?"

She looks taken aback by my booming voice for a moment before she takes another sip of wine. "It means we're adults. We live in the real world and not a fantasy."

"You've slept with other men while we've been together?"

She stands up, letting the blanket drop to the chair. "Please stop being dramatic. I really didn't think you'd care."

I gape at her. "You didn't think I would care that my girlfriend was fucking other men?"

Her nose crinkles. "Don't be so crass."

"Crass?" *She's unbelievable.* "You're sleeping with other people. You're cheating on me, and *I'm* crass? Are you insane?"

"Calm down." She steps away from me, taking her phone with her. She moves to sit on the couch now, looking over at me. "We both know what this is, Adrian. So yes, when a man wants to sweep me off my feet for a night or two and you haven't touched me for a while, I let myself get swept away into a stupid fantasy."

I sit on the same couch, but with plenty of space between us. "I thought we were together."

"We are." Her eyes plead with me. "Because *our parents* want us together. Because it's sensible, and we enjoy each other's company. We're together."

"It's a business arrangement."

She sighs softly and then shrugs. "Yeah, I guess. So, you don't have to worry about finding other women attractive and doing what you want. I just don't want to be like my mom, a quiet little mouse whose husband has many affairs while she sits at home waiting for him."

"You know, you could have let me in on this three years ago." And I would have told her "Hell, no" then.

*Or would I have?*

God, I've become so resigned to just living my life and going along. I probably wouldn't have said a thing.

"I thought we were in a silent agreement. I never, in a million years, thought you would be faithful to me. I mean, I know your father."

I cringe. "I'm not him."

She doesn't argue, but I don't think she believes me either. And why should she? I've never once stood up to him. Never argued. Always been the good boy, just going along.

I stand up. "I can't do this." Adrenaline washes over me because I can't. I don't want to anymore. I want no part of this fucking freak show, trying to parade around as normal. This is not normal.

"Can't do what?" She stands up, looking genuinely confused.

"This. With you. With my parents. Pretending that I'm okay with this life. I'm not."

She snorts at that, dismissing me. "This is our life. You're just going to walk away? Don't be silly, Adrian."

I think back to being eighteen and having the same conversation in my head. Convincing myself that this life is all I'm capable of. "Yeah. I'm going to walk away. I don't want this. I'm a shell of a person."

She studies my face closely. "Adrian, just breathe. I think maybe you had too much to drink. Your father would kill you if you broke it off with me. And I need you."

"You don't though. You're a successful woman, Samantha. You did that on your own."

I see unshed tears form in her eyes as she swallows, her delicate throat moving with the motion. "I didn't. We both know the only reason I gained followers was because of my last name. We were both born with privileges beyond most people's imagination."

"Maybe at the beginning. But you worked hard, and you built up your following on your own. You think even half of your followers give a damn about politics? Hell, if they bothered to research your father, they would probably unfollow you in a heartbeat."

"Don't be cruel." That is her greatest fear. Becoming irrelevant.

"I'm not trying to be. We were born into this life, but we're adults. We need to make our own way."

She shakes her head and wipes a tear from her cheek. I've never seen her cry. "It's not that simple."

"It can be."

"What are you going to do, Adrian? Truly. Think about it. You're a Walker. From generations of political men. It's in your blood. You have no other worldly skills. What on earth are you going to do? Work retail?" She points a finger in my face. "You wouldn't survive. You're used to the finer things, and don't you dare judge me."

"I'm not judging you. And you're right. It would be a struggle, but at least it would be mine." I start toward the door, unsure of where I'm going, but letting my legs carry me away for the first time.

"Adrian." She walks closer to me, the pleading rising in her voice. "You can't do this to me. Just sleep on it."

I shake my head at her. "I don't want to. I've been sleeping through my whole life."

"You're drunk."

"I'm not." Whatever I had earlier is long out of my system.

"Where are you going?"

"I don't know," I say with a smile because it feels good not to have a plan.

"You can't leave me. Just please. We'll talk about it in the morning, okay?"

I shake my head. "It's over, Samantha. It never even really started, but it's over now."

"Please don't go."

I open the door and walk out into the cold, still wearing the robe and slippers, freezing and having no clue where I'm going for the night but not caring. I close the door behind me and start walking.

*I feel guilty, and part of me knows I'll be back in the morning to talk to her. To give her closure, but I also know that I really am done.*

I MAKE THE USUAL ROUNDS, making sure everything is put away and turned off for the day when something catches my eye from the hot tub area on the back deck. I huff, exhausted and wanting this damn day to end as I make my way over there.

I'm back in jeans, t-shirt, and my coat after the disastrous hot tub party. So thank God, I'm not freezing my ass off anymore. As I approach the hot tubs, I do a double take, certain my eyes are playing a trick on me.

"Adrian?"

He turns to look at me and then huffs out a quick, humorless laugh, his breath visible in the cold night air.

I walk closer and see he's sitting on one of the deck chairs, still in his white robe and slippers with a bottle of tequila in his hand.

"What are you doing out here?"

He takes a swig of the alcohol and then holds it out to me. I shake my head no, and he takes another drink. "She thought I stayed behind to fuck Tammy."

"What?" I'm cautious as I approach him and take the seat next to him.

"Samantha." He still won't look at me, his hazels aiming at the trees beyond. "She thought I didn't walk back with her to the cabin because I wanted to hook up with your friend Tammy."

I try to process that. "Did you tell her you didn't?"

He laughs again, without any joy whatsoever. "Yeah. But here's the thing, Nash . . ." Now his eyes meet mine, and I can see they're tired and red from lack of sleep, the cold, and the alcohol. "She didn't care. She wasn't mad at all."

My brows scrunch together. "What do you mean? She wasn't mad? She thought you were cheating."

He shrugs and takes another healthy swig. He wipes at his mouth and shakes his head. "Apparently we're in an open relationship. But I had no fucking idea." He chuckles coldly. "No clue. She's been fucking guys on the side for three years."

*Jesus.* "Adrian . . ."

He takes another drink, and I'm not sure what his tolerance is, but any human would need to slow down. "It doesn't matter. It's all a joke. I mean, you know that better than anyone, right?"

"I don't know that."

He looks out at the trees again. "Yeah, you do. I've barely touched her. And when I did, I needed liquid courage and to shut my eyes to conjure up a fantasy."

"You're going to regret these words tomorrow."

His eyes meet mine again, burning through me. "No. I won't. Because it's true. And how can anyone regret the truth?"

I study him. He looks so damn tired. So broken. Maybe it should bring me some joy, but it doesn't. I hate it for him. "What's your truth, Adrian?"

"I'm tired of being someone I'm not."

I swallow thickly, knowing these are words fueled by alcohol and maybe even some heartbreak. But still, a little glimmer of hope blooms deep down inside, and I try to push it away.

*He's the boy who left you looking like an idiot.*

"I don't love her. I know she's beautiful. And she's driven. But we're too much alike. We were both raised with a silver spoon in our mouths that we could keep as long as we towed the line."

I don't want to feel sorry for him. "I'm sure you guys can work it out."

He laughs and takes another drink. "No. I'm done. She's fucking other people and totally fine with me doing the same. It's ridiculous."

"Won't your father be mad?"

"Oh, he'll try every trick in the book to get me to fix it." He leans back, his throat stretched tight as he looks up at the sky. "I don't care anymore."

*I doubt that.*

I don't call him out on it though. "So, you never . . ." He lifts his head and looks at me, one eyebrow raised as he waits. "You never cheated on her?"

"No. Not once. I thought we were exclusive." He snorts. "I'm an idiot."

*He's so damn hard on himself. Goddammit. I don't care.*

I sigh. "You can't stay out here all night. You're not even dressed."

He holds up the bottle. "Tequila keeps you warm. Did you know that?"

"No. It doesn't protect you from hypothermia. Go back to your girlfriend, Adrian."

I stand up, but he stands too. Although, he does it a little too fast and nearly loses his balance. His hand grabs my shoulder, and the touch sends shockwaves through me that I'm not proud of. I stare at his hand, and his eyes go to the same place. "Sorry."

"It's fine." I clear my throat, hoping he'll pull his hand away, but he doesn't.

"I can't go back there tonight. Please tell me there's another cabin."

Now it's my turn to laugh. I take the tequila bottle and place it down on the bar next to us. "Yeah, no. We're fully booked for months because of your girlfriend."

He doesn't look surprised, only sadly nodding his head and removing his hand, this time keeping his balance. I sigh, taking pity on him I know I shouldn't.

"Come on."

He gazes up at me. "Where?"

"You can stay in my cabin tonight." His eyes turn hopeful. And I swear I see a hint of lust, so I quickly add, "On the couch."

His face drops, but he nods and follows me through the woods to my cabin. When we get inside, I start a fire in the fireplace as he sits down on the couch. I nod to the back of the sofa. "There's a blanket you can use. It'll take a bit to warm up in here."

He does that, pulling the throw blanket off the couch and throwing it over his shoulders. "So, you and Hayden aren't together?"

I hear the vulnerability in his voice and feel bad about letting him believe that. "No. We aren't. Why? You interested?" I turn to look at him, actually hating that question and how much jealousy I feel, even knowing Hayden would never do that to me.

"Not in him."

*Damn. It.*

I turn away, going back to the fire, knowing he doesn't mean it. "You'll make up with Samantha tomorrow."

"No. I won't."

I get the fire going and sit down on the chair, situated opposite to the couch. Best to keep my distance. He looks cold and vulnerable, so damn lost but also—oddly—confident.

"We never had sex."

"What?"

"Samantha and me. I convinced her that since our relationship was the endgame, heading toward marriage, that we should wait. So, I never had sex with her. Not one time, and she still thought I was out fucking other women." His fingers rake through his thick hair.

"That's . . ." I don't know what that is. *Sad? Odd?*

"I know. It's fucked up. It's all so confusing."

"You're going to hate every part of this conversation tomorrow." I lean back in the chair. "She was raised the same way as you, right?" He nods. "She's probably just scared."

He agrees. "Oh, she is. She's terrified of becoming her mother. Waiting at home for me as I fuck my way through the state."

I stand up and remove my coat, trying to ignore his gaze that's plastered to me. "You should get some sleep. Do you need to borrow some clothes?"

He nods his head thankfully. "Yes, please."

I go into my room and then bring him a pair of sweats and a t-shirt, knowing both will be too big for him, but they should work for the night. "Goodnight."

He stands up, and his cold hand reaches out and grabs my wrist, stopping me from my escape. "I'm glad you've been free."

He's standing too close to me. Even with his eyes all bloodshot and him being full of alcohol, he smells good. He looks good. And I can't do this.

I want to say so many things. That I haven't felt free at all. That I've been trapped by his memory. But I don't.

"Goodnight, Adrian."

He removes his hand. "Goodnight, Nash."

I leave, forcing my feet to carry me to my room and close the door.

*Whether he's with Samantha or not, I'm not sliding back into these games with him.*

# Adrian

My head is going to explode. I'm certain of that. If I open my eyes, my head will actually explode all over the place.

*Why did I drink so much?*

I groan and roll to my side on the uncomfortable sofa. *Why am I on the couch?*

"Morning."

*Fuck!* I sit up way too fast at the sound of Nash's voice. All of it comes rushing back as the world around me spins.

*Oh my God. I said way too much last night. Way, way too much.*

Nash looks concerned and slightly amused as he stands before me, wearing a pair of low-slung jeans and nothing else. Jesus, he's ripped now. Every single ab muscle is defined and pronounced. His pecs are hardened with a light dusting of dark hair. And that beard is drool-worthy all on its own.

I've been staring at him way too long. I look down at the sweats I borrowed from him last night and try not to look at him again. "Here." *Damn it.* I look up at the sound of his voice and only now notice he's holding out a white mug full of coffee to me. "Maybe it will help."

I take the mug from his hands, but I don't drink. "I don't think anything will help."

"Yeah. Hangovers are the worst."

This is awkward.

"Nash," I start but don't know where I'm going with this. His dark eyes meet mine.

"I know. You need to go back to your girl."

I shake my head, a little too fast, sending the world spinning again, and my stomach lurches. I put the mug down and rush for the bathroom, covering my mouth with my hand and praying I make it there.

Thankfully, I do before I lose the half bottle of tequila in the toilet. This morning just went from awkward to humiliating. When I'm finished, I flush and wipe my mouth with the back of my hand. Nash stands in the doorway, nodding his head to the sink. "There's an extra toothbrush."

I can't look at him. I admitted way too many things to him last night.

"Thank you."

I wash my hands and then my mouth out, spitting into the sink and then grab the extra toothbrush to brush properly. I feel like shit but a little better after vomiting.

"It'll get better."

I don't know if he's talking about my hangover or my life. But at the moment, I'm not sure he'd be right about either. I spit into the sink and wash my mouth out again with water. I place the toothbrush back on the sink and turn to him. "I'm not going back to Samantha. At least, not to get back together."

He doesn't believe me. That much is clear by the expression on his face. "Just go talk to her."

"I don't want that life, Nash."

He nearly takes up the entire doorway of the bathroom, his large body crowding the small space as he stares at me, his gaze unreadable. "We'll see."

He turns to leave, but I follow him, reaching out and catching his wrist in my hand. He spins around to look at me, and for a moment I'm stunned stupid at his close proximity to me. "I'm serious."

He leans in a little closer. Giving me a whiff of something woodsy and so damn sexy. *Cologne? Maybe. Possibly beard oil. Whatever it is, it's working.* "I've heard that before."

"I was a kid," I try to defend, but it's weak.

"So was I."

"I know." I look away, but I don't relinquish my hold on his arm. I can't offer an explanation. "I'm going to talk to her, but it's over. I ended it with her."

He pulls his arm away from me, but he doesn't walk away. "And what then? Your father is going to have a fit."

"I don't care." My words are surprisingly firm.

But Nash still laughs, although humorlessly. "You do. But seriously, Adrian. What are you going to do? You break up with her, and then what happens?"

"I don't know." I haven't had much time to think about it. And even less of that time has been sober. "I just know I can't keep sleepwalking through my life, playing a part."

He walks away from me now, shaking his head, and I follow him into the bedroom. He seems annoyed but doesn't tell me to leave. He only walks over to his closet and pulls a green polo out, pulling it on over his head. "Don't burn down your entire life unless you're certain."

"You're different."

The words escape me before I can stop them, and his eyes bore into me from across the room. "How?"

Well, the words were already spoken and despite the throbbing headache, I might as well just go with it. "You used to tell me I was more than that life. That I should leave it behind and be me. Now, you're telling me to what . . . stay in the closet? Stay with Samantha?"

He walks closer to me now. "I'm not telling you to do anything. It's none of my business."

For whatever the reason, the words sting. "You're saying not to burn my life to the ground?"

"Unless you're sure." He leans in close, his red lips peeking out through the thick beard and causing me to get lost for a moment. His dark eyes search mine. "And you aren't."

"Don't tell me what I am and what I'm not, Nash."

A smirk plays on his lips as he cocks his head to the side. "Did you finally grow a pair?"

"I've always had them," I bite out.

"Just never used them."

I don't look away. I'm tired of being afraid. "I am now."

He deflates slightly, his shoulders going slack as he sighs and shakes his head. "I pushed you too much when we were young. You were scared, and I shouldn't have pressured you to come out. It wasn't up to me."

My mouth opens to say something but then closes again because I didn't expect him to say that. "I made you promises."

"But I knew you were afraid." He lifts a hand to his hair and drags his fingers through it, his bicep flexing to an almost ungodly size, stretching the sleeve of his polo. I'm mesmerized by the action. "That's why I'm saying you need to be sure now. That you're doing what you want to."

"I am." I step even closer to him, our bare feet touching, and I place my hand over his heart, just feeling the rapid thump, thump, thump under my palm. "I can't live like this anymore."

"No one should have to." His voice is gravelly and so damn sexy. I close my eyes and just feel. I breathe him in and go back to the last time I felt like me, like an actual human. In his arms, making plans that I'm still pretty sure never would have worked.

"It's over with her."

I feel his nose brush over mine and nearly gasp from the contact, but I don't open my eyes. I don't want this to be my imagination. "You have to be sure."

I take a deep breath in and open my eyes slowly as I release the air from my lungs and look directly into his eyes. "I am."

And then, it's just lips and tongues, colliding together for the first time in years. My hands roam over his solid chest before I grip his polo and drag him closer to me. He groans into my mouth as we kiss, not coming up for air because it feels too good.

His tongue teases mine, fighting for dominance, and I don't give in easily. His hands move to my ass, gripping it as he lifts me, and I wrap my legs around him before my back hits the wall behind us.

Still, we don't stop. I hold onto him for dear life as his mouth ravages mine, and our hard cocks grind together, both begging for relief and so much more time together. I don't ever want to leave this moment.

But I feel him start to pull away from me as the kiss starts to fade, and my mouth chases his, pleading for more time. "Nash," I whisper against his mouth.

His lips withdraw, and his forehead rests against mine as he leaves me pressed between his hard body and the wall at my back. "I can't."

"Please?" I don't care how pathetic I sound. I haven't been touched like this in so long.

He shakes his head, his forehead rubbing against mine with the action. "I can't. You need to go."

He releases me, and I feel coldness seep throughout my entire body as my feet hit the ground and he moves away from me. I stand there for a moment as he sits on the edge of his bed, raking his fingers through his hair and not looking at me.

He doesn't owe me anything. I know that. But the rejection still stings. I silently walk out of his room and don't bother grabbing the robe from last night as I put my feet into the slippers.

I walk outside, the bitter cold hitting my skin, but I barely feel it.

*All I've ever wanted was him.*

# Adrian

I WALK BACK into the cabin I've shared with Samantha, wearing Nash's clothes, my lips still swollen from our kiss. Samantha walks into the living room, fully dressed as her eyes swipe over my appearance.

And I'm sure I'm quite the sight.

"Do you feel better?"

I quirk an eyebrow in her direction, certain I don't look like I feel good at all. "I feel like shit. I'm hungover. And tired." *Rejected.* But I don't add that last thought.

She waves me off and sits down on the couch, phone in hand. "Well, good. Maybe a good night of debauchery is what you needed to relax."

I sit down next to her, leaving plenty of space and running my fingers through my hair. "I don't need to relax. I meant what I said, Samantha. This thing with us is over."

Her eyes meet mine, and for once, I see actual emotion there. Anger. "We are not over. Don't be ridiculous. We had a fight."

"We don't care about each other enough to fight."

"That's just . . ." She huffs and folds her arms. "That's not true."

"It is. I do care about you, Samantha. In the sense that I don't want anything bad to happen to you, but I don't love you."

She snorts and rolls her eyes. "Don't be ridiculous. I know that." Her hand moves to my knee. "It doesn't matter to me. But we can't break up, and you know it."

"I don't know that."

She's becoming increasingly annoyed with me now as she looks up at the ceiling and takes a deep breath before her eyes level with mine. "You do know that. Your dad will disown you at this point if you don't propose." It doesn't surprise me in the slightest that she knows about the proposal. "My parents will be angry. It will be more trouble than it's worth, Adrian." She waves her hand. "I already told you, you can sleep with whoever you want on the side. Just be discreet, and make sure you're home more often than not."

"You think that's a life? Just barely living? Having affairs and then coming home to your spouse, having polite conversation, and then going to bed feeling empty? That's what you want?"

"You're acting far more naïve than you really are, Adrian. I'm tired of this. We both knew what this was when our parents introduced us. We're a great fit. My followers love us together. And they, along with all the voters, are salivating for our marriage. Then our kids."

I stand up, frustrated with the entire conversation. Frustrated with this life that I've lived, blindly going along with everything because that's the way things are done. "You would bring kids into this?"

Her nose scrunches up a little as she seems to think it over before shrugging. "Sure. Why not? They'd be very lucky to grow up the way we have. The best of the best. Best home. Best vacations. Best schools. Best life."

"Money doesn't equal the best life." She stands up, one hand on her hip.

"What has gotten into you? I don't understand. Did you watch some weird indie movie or something?"

I stare at her, trying to find an ounce of the humanity I thought I saw in her. "I've been numb. And stupid. I don't want this anymore. I'm not doing it. You and I are over."

"No, we aren't. You need me, Adrian. As much as I need you."

"I don't."

"You can sleep with whoever you want. I don't care if you more than likely shared your bed with Tammy last night. Okay? I don't care."

"Jesus Christ," I growl, losing my patience. "I wasn't with Tammy last night. I'm not interested in Tammy."

She rolls her eyes, dismissing me. "Fine. Whoever you shared a bed with. I don't care."

"Exactly," I throw out. "You don't care. And *I* don't care. It should have infuriated me that you were letting other men inside you, but it didn't. Not at all. I. Don't. Care."

"So, what is the problem?"

*How is she this clueless? How have I allowed this to go this far?* "I'm gay."

The words leave my mouth, tumbling out before I can overthink it or pull it back. I don't want to though. The words feel so good coming out of my mouth I actually laugh. I'm not sure if it's necessarily joy, but it's close. I feel a sort of euphoria and disbelief, mixed together, that I came out and said it.

"That's not funny."

I school my features and take a deep breath, making sure my face conveys just how serious I am. "No, it's not. It's not supposed to be. I am gay."

"Stop saying that."

She looks nearly disgusted now. Her face scrunched up. "It's the truth."

"No, it's not." She folds her arms over her stomach, looking like she may be sick. "You can't be gay." Her gaze spears through me. "Your father will kill you."

"I don't think he'll actually go that far."

Her eyes search mine. "You are not gay."

I step closer to her, certain she's in shock. I can't blame her for that. We've been together for three years. It wasn't fair to her. I know that. "I am."

I place a hand on her shoulder, hoping to offer some comfort, but she jerks away from me. "Don't touch me."

"What?"

"Don't you dare tell me that you're gay and then touch me."

"I wasn't trying to do anything—"

She cuts me off, "But you have. You've kissed me, Adrian." Shame washes over me, and my eyes flutter closed involuntarily at the thought that I've used her. I open them, and she's still glaring at me. "You've done more than kiss me. And . . ." Her eyes drop lower, down to my crotch. "I've felt you."

I know I need to tread carefully here. "I know . . ." I run my fingers through my hair and try like hell to choose my words with enough thought before I say them. "It's a physical response to being touched. And you're beautiful . . . I just . . ."

"Oh my god, when I went down on you, were you pretending I was a man?" She looks horrified, covering her mouth with one hand. "Is that what you did?"

"No. I didn't really allow myself to think about anything."

"I don't look anything like a man, Adrian. I am very much a woman, and you were hard. You finished. I . . ." She tosses her hand in the air. "You are not gay."

"Yes, I am." I say it firmly because it doesn't matter if I could physically get off on occasion with her. I'm not attracted to her. I don't fantasize about women and their soft curves. It takes a hard, masculine body to truly get me aroused. "I know this is confusing, and I shouldn't have kept it from you."

"You lied to me. You let me . . ." Tears well up in her eyes. "This is not okay. You touched me, not even being remotely attracted to me?"

"You're very beautiful."

"Stop saying that," she snaps. "You don't actually want to fuck me."

"No," I say softly.

She sits back down on the couch and takes in a deep breath. I'm not sure what she's thinking exactly, but I know her well enough to know thoughts are swirling around in her head. "Okay."

"Okay?" I study her carefully, waiting for more.

"Yeah. Okay. So, you're gay. Whatever. That doesn't mean we have to break up."

I stare at her stupidly, unmoving. "It's exactly what that means."

"No." She waves me off easily. "So, you don't sleep with me. Fine. I can deal with that. We've never had sex anyway."

I shake my head. "No. I don't want to be in a loveless marriage."

She laughs at me, and it's cruel. "Grow up, Adrian. Love is for movies and books, not us."

I think about that kiss with Nash earlier and close my eyes, remembering his touch. Remembering way before when he would look into my eyes and awake every nerve in my body. "That's not true. And I'm not doing this."

I start for the door, but she jumps up and grabs my hand. "Adrian, what are you planning to do? Just go out there and live some great big gay life?"

She sounds horrified, but I only smirk. "That actually sounds great."

Her jaw drops, and she releases me, stepping away. "You can't do that to me."

"Do what to you?"

Her face is full of hurt and horror. "If you . . ." She looks like she's searching for the right words and lands on, "come out, everyone will think it's my fault."

*Jesus fucking Christ.* "It's no one's 'fault.' It's nothing to be ashamed of. And I've lived far too long believing that bullshit. I don't care what anyone thinks."

"Well, you should care. They are going to annihilate us both for this. But they're going to say that I turned you gay."

I take a step closer to her, my jaw tightening. "That's ridiculous, and deep down, you know that. Everyone knows that. You can't make someone gay. I was born attracted to men instead of women. That's it."

Her nose crinkles. "That's not what they'll say."

"I don't care what they say." She flinches when I raise my voice, and I force myself to calm down and back away from her.

"What changed?" She wipes away a tear. "Before we got here, you were a straight man." *I want to bang my head on the wall.*

"I wasn't straight. I was suppressing the hell out of myself and trying to fit into the goddamn box I was born into."

"What changed then? Since we've been here? What the hell changed and made you all of a sudden want to give up everything you've worked for? To give up on us?" Her eyes widen, and now I'm the one who feels sick as her head turns toward the front door of the cabin. "Hayden?"

"What?" I barely choke out.

She covers her mouth again and looks at me, shaking her head. "Oh my God. You're sleeping with Hayden. That's why."

"No," I say firmly. "I'm not."

I move toward her again, pleading with my eyes for her to understand me, but she backs away just shaking her head. "We need to go. I can't be here if that's the kind of people we'll be around. We have to pack up and get out of here. I need to make a post." She takes out her phone, and I think my heart may stop for a minute.

"No," I nearly shout, making her stop. "Don't do that. I'm not sleeping with Hayden. He's not my type." My type are big, burly sexy bearded men. Or man. I don't say that though.

"Don't lie to me."

"Just a few minutes ago, you were totally fine with me sleeping around."

"Not with a man," she bites out with disgust.

"I'm not. But it shouldn't matter. You're totally fine with me fucking around. And I wasn't. Don't destroy their business with your hateful, ignorant bullshit."

She's angry now as her eyes narrow, and she places a hand on her hip. "Then don't leave. We stay together."

My heart sinks as I realize what she's saying. "No."

She lifts her phone again. "Yes."

"What the hell are you doing? You're going to blackmail me into being in a relationship with you? Are you insane? You can have any man you want, Samantha. You don't have to do that."

Her lower lip quivers, but she must push away the tears because she straightens her shoulders. "I know we won't actually be a couple, but I need the illusion. If you leave me and start sleeping with men, my image will shatter."

"No." I shake my head, "No. I won't give up my life for your image anymore. I won't."

She huffs, her foot tapping on the wood floor of the cabin. "Two months."

"What?" I stare at her, dumbfounded.

"Give me two more months. And I'll give this place a raving review. For whatever reason, you seem to be very interested in them doing well. Even though you claim to not have a thing for Hayden."

I shake my head again, but it's slower. "What the hell difference does two months make?"

"I can prepare myself and my followers for us parting ways amicably."

"No, Samantha. It doesn't change anything. I can't do this." Not even for Nash. For his brother's business.

I start toward the door, but her voice stops me again. I expect venom but what I hear is vulnerability. "Please. Just give me time to tell my dad first. This will kill him, and he's not well."

Yeah, no shit. He's a homophobic asshole. I turn to look at her. "You really think me being gay is going to kill him?"

"It could," she snaps and looks like a little girl pouting. "Please, Adrian. You owe me a little more time. I haven't been alone in three years."

My shoulders sag. "You don't need me."

"I wish that wasn't true. But I do. Please just give me time. Don't tell anyone yet. You've been hiding this your whole life. What's two more months?"

Two more months of not being the true me seems like a lifetime. It doesn't make sense because she's right, I've hidden it for so long. But now that it's out . . .

*How can I reel it back in?*

"No. I don't . . ."

"Adrian, please. It's the holidays. I need pictures with my boyfriend." Her expression turns slightly sinister. "In this beautiful place that seems to have really increased in business since we've been here."

I glare at her, but maybe deep down, I know I owe Nash. It's never going to be enough for what I did to him, but maybe, just maybe, me being here and keeping Samantha happy will make up for it a little bit.

"Fine."

She smiles happily and then holds up her phone, going to my side. "Smile pretty." Her lips press against my cheek, but I don't bother smiling as the flash nearly blinds me, not helping the hangover in the slightest.

*Lawson means the world to Nash.*

*I can do this for him.*

# Nash

I'M STILL REELING from my conversation with Adrian earlier, but that doesn't mean I can take the day off. There are things to be done, and I'm grateful. Keeping busy has always helped me. After cutting firewood and piling it up nicely outside, I head into the dining hall to see if anyone needs help with the breakfast buffet.

I find Hayden sitting at one of the tables, his phone in hand, and sit across from him. The place is packed with mostly families, grabbing breakfast. Hayden looks bright and cheery for having had a margarita party last night and indulging in a few.

"Morning, sunshine! Wanna see your boyfriend's newest post?"

I tense and keep my voice low. "He's not my boyfriend."

He holds his phone up for me to see. "He's not hers either."

I look at the photo, seeing what I know is a very hungover Adrian, his hair messed from sleep, and maybe a little from our kiss, and a grumpy expression as Samantha presses a kiss to his cheek. She's captioned it, *"When your man isn't a morning person, you just have to give him a little love."* And it's already gained quite a bit of swooning attention.

I grunt in frustration but try not to give anything away. "They look together to me."

Hayden waves me off. "Please. Their relationship is faker than fake. And that boy is still totally in love with you."

My chest actually aches with his words, and I wince. His

expression softens, and he puts his phone down, reaching across the table to place a hand over mine.

"I'm sorry."

"It's fine. If that's the life he wants, then it's up to him. He's a big boy." *But he said he didn't want that life.*

I try to push my thoughts away. I can't trust him. That's all there is to it.

Proof of that comes walking through the door only a second later. Samantha walks in with confidence and a wide smile, dressed impeccably with her arm locked around Adrian's. He looks a little more disheveled but subtly. He's not in my clothes now. Instead, he's dressed in khakis and a sweater, his hair washed and styled, but his eyes are still red.

He looks like he feels like shit, and I don't know if it's from the hangover or our morning together. Maybe from facing his soon-to-be fiancé. It's clear they're still together, though, as they greet Rae and Lawson, both with smiles on their faces as Samantha leans into his body.

I'm such a fucking idiot.

I kissed him. And even though the kiss was totally mutual, I initiated it. I pressed my lips against his and gave into the desire coursing through me.

"You're staring." Hayden's voice is kind and cautious as he quietly warns me about my own actions.

I jerk my eyes away from the happy couple and meet his eyes that are sad and full of pity for me. "Thanks."

"Did something happen last night after I left?" He's not digging for gossip. That much I know about him. He truly cares and he's intuitive as hell.

"No. Not really. He got really drunk, and I let him sleep it off at my place."

"Oh?" He's smiling playfully now.

"Nothing happened." Not really. It's not like it matters when he's playing house with Travel Barbie over there. I risk a glance at them and see they're still talking to Rae and Law. He's not pulling out of her hold.

I grimace and look back over at Hayden, who's shaking his head at me with a smile still firmly on his lips. "You know you can tell me anything." His face turns slightly more serious as he lowers his voice even further. "And Adrian already knows I know about the two of you. You can talk to me if you need to, Nash."

I sigh, pulling in a deep breath and letting it out because I know that's true. And I'm so damn tired of living with secrets. "We kissed. Nothing else happened, and I told him to leave."

Sadness fills his eyes as he touches my hand and squeezes. "And now, he's here with her like nothing happened." It's not a question as he shakes his head solemnly and takes his hand away. "That must hurt like hell."

*It does. It shouldn't. He's not mine and hasn't been for a long time. Hell, maybe he never was. He is hers though.* "It doesn't feel great."

He looks over at Adrian and then looks back to me. "I kind of pity him, you know? I could have been him."

"What do you mean?"

He shrugs his small shoulders. "I was born into a pretty similar life of the rich and privileged. When I came out, they were so mad, but they still wanted me to play their part." He laughs, but I hear the pain in his words. "As if I could ever play straight."

"No one should ever have to *play* anything in real life."

His smile brightens a little now as he sits up a little straighter. "I agree. I've found my people, but maybe Adrian hasn't had that."

"He had me," I snap maybe a little too heatedly, but Hayden is unbothered.

"Yeah. But we don't get to choose other people's paths. He wasn't ready."

"I don't think he'll ever be ready."

He looks sympathetic. "Then, fuck him." I raise an eyebrow, and he giggles, waving me off. "Not literally. I mean . . ." He glances over at Adrian and then back at me. "Maybe literally. He's in the closet, not you."

I shake my head. "I'm not touching him again. Not while he's still playing his role."

He looks deep in thought for a moment and then sighs softly. "Maybe all he needs is to see what life could be like, Nash. The people he could be surrounded with. Where he doesn't have to hide."

I try to swallow the lump that's formed in my throat. Thinking about the possibility of him staying here. Of laughter-filled dinners with Rae, Law, Tammy, and Hayden. Of going back to our cabin and kissing him whenever I wanted.

I push it away.

I always push it away because that isn't reality. He'll be gone in a couple of weeks. He'll walk out of my life and back into life with her, having quiet dinners and sharing kisses that don't feel quite right because they aren't.

I stand up abruptly. "I have to go. If anyone needs anything done, give me a call."

I don't give him a chance to console me and head outside as quickly as I can, not looking at Adrian and Samantha.

But it's only a moment after I get outside that I hear the door open and close behind me, and I know before I even turn around that Adrian is behind me. I close my eyes and take a deep breath, not wanting to face him.

He makes me weak and stupid.

Neither are good things. "Go back in there."

"No."

I turn around to face him angrily. "Goddammit, Adrian. Go back in there."

He walks closer to me, out here in the open, but he seems determined to get near me. "No."

"It's clear you're still with her."

"I'm not."

I laugh without humor, and it comes out with fury. "Stop lying to me." I raise one hand in the air with frustration. "Hell, stop lying to yourself. That post this morning? You and her coming to breakfast together. You are very much together."

We're standing so close, his shoes touch mine, but he doesn't move away. He only looks firmly into my eyes. "We aren't. I told her this morning."

"Told her what? That you think you want waffles? Maybe try an omelet?"

He actually smiles at that and goddamn, it's beautiful. Everything about Adrian is so damn beautiful. "No, smartass." His voice is a little quieter now, but it's not a whisper. "That I'm gay."

I stare at him in shock. "What?"

His smile only broadens, and it makes my stupid heart beat more rapidly in my chest, filling with godforsaken hope that is beyond dangerous. "I did."

I squash the hope. "That sure doesn't explain why you're here with her this morning, playing her little dutiful boyfriend."

His eyes darken slightly now, and he nods. "Meet me later."

It's not a question, more a bold command. "No." My voice isn't nearly as sure, and I curse myself for it.

"Please, Nash."

His eyes plead with mine. "Fine. Come to my cabin. I'm assuming it'll have to be after dark, so you can sneak away."

He only smirks at me, not impacted by me being an asshole. And he does seem different in a way I can't quite figure out. "Okay. I'll be there."

*Damn. It.*

# Adrian

I SPENT most of my day working and avoiding Samantha. I'll play the part in public right now to appease her, but I'm definitely not doing it behind closed doors. She's spent a lot of the day on social media and ignoring my existence too.

For dinner, we went to a restaurant in town, and I posed for her pictures. But now that we're back and there are no more plans for the night, I head for the front door with my coat on.

"Where are you going?" I didn't think she'd even notice, and she doesn't look up from her phone when she asks.

"Out."

"Out where?" Her tone is sharp, and she's glaring at me now.

"Wherever I want. I don't owe you any explanations. We aren't together."

It feels good to say that, like a weight has lifted off my chest despite her pissy attitude. "You still have to be discreet, Adrian. No," she lowers her voice to nearly a whisper and looks around as if someone could be hiding in here somewhere, "gay clubs or anything."

I roll my eyes at her. "Do you know of any around here?"

She huffs. "Of course not."

"Damn." I'm fucking with her, but I'm sick of her attitude. "How about this? You mind your damn business, and I'll give you a few more weeks of this bullshit façade. But I don't want to hear any more of your vile opinions about gay people."

"It's not gay people, Adrian. It's my future fiancé being gay. Or saying that he is as some sort of . . ." she waves her hand in the air, looking for the word, "I don't know, quarter-life crisis?"

I grab the door handle, not really wanting to engage with her any more than I need to. "Call it what you want." I smile. "I'm gay. And I'm not ashamed of it anymore."

I walk outside, closing the door behind me and not wanting to hear anything else from her. Not wanting any part of my old life, but I do know I need to keep her happy, for the most part. I can't let her do anything to harm Lawson and Raelynn's business.

I make my way to Nash's cabin and knock as soon as I get there so I don't lose my nerve. He opens it almost immediately, but he still looks surprised that I'm here. And he looks damn good in tight jeans and a black t-shirt, the fire roaring in the fireplace behind him. "Hi."

It's stupid. But it's really all I can come up with right now. "You're here."

"I am." I nod dumbly. "Can I come in?"

He only crosses his massive arms, making the muscles pop even more. "What does your girlfriend think of you being here?"

"She hates it. But I couldn't care less since she's not my girlfriend."

He quirks a dark eyebrow, studying me, but not moving out of my way either. I know this has to be bizarre to him. Hell, it's strange for me too. It's like I was drowning for so damn long, gasping for air and not getting it. Now, I've gotten one small ounce of air into my lungs, and I'm breathing again.

I'm alive, and I don't ever want to go back.

"Please let me come in, Nash. I want to explain everything."

He drops his arms in a huff and moves out of the doorway, letting me inside his home. He closes the door behind him and turns toward me, making it hard for me to think with him this close to me. I should explain everything, going all the way back to when we were eighteen. But all I can do is take in the beautiful sight of Nash before me.

"Explain." His voice is deep and a strong command.

"Which part?" I ask carefully because I want to know what he wants to hear.

"How about the part where you told your soon-to-be fiancé you're gay and then ended up playing happy couple at breakfast?" He takes a step closer to me, and I breathe him in greedily. His eyes dart over my face and land on my eyes. "The same morning you kissed me in this very cabin."

I swallow thickly, thinking about that kiss this morning and trying to tell my cock to calm down long enough to talk. Talking. That's what I'm supposed to be doing. Not thinking about his soft but firm lips on mine and the way he held me against the wall.

"Adrian."

Right. Focus. "That's complicated." He shakes his head and starts to walk away from me, but I grab his elbow to stop him. "Complicated, but I'll explain."

He stops trying to walk away, his expression dark and disbelieving. "Then do it."

I clear my throat, uncertain where to start, and I release his arm because I can't think with any part of me touching any part of him. "I told her again this morning when I got back that I didn't want to be with her. And she just went on and on about how she doesn't care if I'm with other people but that I need her and she needs me."

"For political reasons?"

I nod, knowing how stupid it seems. "Societal. Our families expect us to be together. Their voters want us together. Her followers."

"Everyone but you."

I agree, "I told her I didn't want that anymore, that I was leaving. And again, she told me how little she cared about what I did." I swallow away the bile trying to rise in my throat, just thinking about the whole conversation. "I told her I'm gay. I said the words out loud."

That smile comes back to my face, and I can feel Nash's eyes on my mouth as it does. "And what did she say?"

I frown. "She was awful. Extremely. Just disgusting."

His jaw ticks with barely contained anger. "And yet, you agreed to go to breakfast with her."

"There's more to it than that."

115

"Like what?" His voice raises now, and I don't blame him at all for being angry.

I step closer to him, searching his eyes, and I reach out, brushing my hand over the soft hair over his cheek. "If I don't play her games, she'll leave, Nash." He looks confused, our eyes locked. "She'll leave this place and probably make up some nasty bullshit reason for leaving. One that could really hurt the business."

Realization dawns on him, and I can see it in his eyes. "She's what? Blackmailing you?"

I smooth my hand over his cheek, loving the feeling of his coarse beard. "I guess. In a way. Although I told her I wasn't doing it for long. But I can't let her tank this place. I know it means the world to you all."

"So, what are you going to do? Play her boyfriend during the day, and then what, Adrian?" He moves in so his lips are near mine, making me whimper embarrassingly. "Fuck me at night?"

I lick my lips, suddenly dry from longing as I look at his luscious lips peeking out from his beard and oh, so close to mine. "I'm not playing anything anymore. I'll take her stupid pictures, but that's it. I don't act like a boyfriend in private."

"Have you ever?" he questions.

I lift my chin a little in defiance, knowing he's calling me out. "Fine, I've played the part in the past in private as well as out in the open, but I'm done with that. When she checks out of here, she's going alone. I'm done with her."

"You really think whatever time you have left here will be enough for her? For your father?"

"I don't care anymore, Nash. I just don't."

He steps away from me, the distance sending an ache through me. "Then why go along with it at all?"

"I told you. She'll leave."

"Do you really think I care?" He's angry.

"Yes. I do." I look out the window, seeing the snow starting to fall and then look back at Nash. "I know you care about your brother more than anything. I know this place is important."

"They were doing fine without her."

"But aren't they doing phenomenally now?" I cross my arms, pissed at him for being pissed at me. Which makes no sense, but whatever. "They can do even better. This can set them up for life."

"At what expense?"

A sadness flows through me like I've known for so long. The kind of sadness you only feel when you're hiding who you really are inside. Of living a lie. "I can do this. I want to do this."

"Of course, you do."

Now, I'm really pissed at the implication. "What the hell is that supposed to mean? You think I want to live my life another second in the closet? After I've found the freedom of saying the words out loud? After I know that insanely good feeling?" I move closer to him. "You think I want that?"

He stares down at me, his few inches on me giving him the height advantage. "Yes."

I glare at him, our chests heaving and brushing together with every breath. "Fuck you."

"You're telling me that after years of hiding, you come here, and all a sudden, you're just out?"

"That's how it happens sometimes, asshole." I'm angry, my hands clenching into fists at my sides.

"I call bullshit. I think you want to hide. That you're scared."

"What do I have to do, Nash? Huh? What do I have to do to prove to you that I really am done with all the hiding bullshit? That I want to really be me. The real me that only you know."

I don't get a chance to say anything else as his strong hand grabs the back of my neck and pulls me in for a kiss that's so intense, I gasp against his lips before I fall into the movement of our mouths. He sucks on my tongue when I slide it into his mouth, and I groan, wanting so many things all at once.

My fingers dig into his hips, pulling him flush against me so I can feel his erection rubbing against mine. His mouth devours mine as we move backwards. My back hits the wall, and I moan into his mouth, "Please. Please don't stop."

I can feel his conflict. "We talk later."

I nod in agreement. I'm sure I'll agree to anything in this moment if he'll just keep kissing me. Which he does. We kiss and kiss until my lips are nearly numb, and I feel like I could come in my pants just doing this, but I want so much more.

My hands smooth under his shirt, relishing every single dip and valley of his sculpted abs, and he moans into my mouth at the contact. "I've missed you," I mumble against his lips. "So damn much." I move back down and find the button of his jeans, undoing it and the zipper quickly.

We both groan when I palm his hardened cock through his boxer briefs. "Jesus."

I smile at the word sounding like a curse from his lips and dip into the briefs, feeling the scathing hot velvety skin of his dick, hard and dripping for me. "Please don't stop me."

He shakes his head, both of us too far gone as he undoes my khakis and pushes them down with my briefs in an instant, seemingly impatient. I get the memo and push his pants and underwear down as well and then pull him back to me, kissing him hard.

His hard body against mine is everything I could ever ask for. We rut against each other, enjoying the delicious rhythm of each of our cocks rubbing against the other's.

"Fuck," he gasps and then pulls away from my mouth long enough to bring his hand to his mouth, licking it. I watch in a trance before a long, deep groan escapes my throat when he wraps his big hand around both of us.

"Oh God, Nash." I nip on his jaw, covered by his beard and then move back to his lips, nibbling the bottom one. "I'm not going to last."

He only grunts, moving his hand over our cocks, slickened by his spit. It's almost too much for me to process as I remain happily trapped between the wall and his large body. He kisses me, covering my mouth as I moan and writhe against him, lost in the moment.

I never want it to end. The fingers of my left hand grasp his hair, and my right hand is on his ass, pulling him into me, begging for more and less all at once because I want this to last. Who knows what will happen after this?

I feel my balls draw up tight and bite his bottom lip again. "I can't . . ." It's useless to fight it, my orgasm beating me to the words as I spill over his hand, his cock jerking with his own release right after. He moves his hand, milking every last drop of cum from us both until my legs are trembling so intensely, I have to beg him to stop.

I look down at the mess between us, our spent cocks covered and sticky with our release, and I rest my head against his chest.

"Let's get cleaned up." I lift my head at Nash's words, our chests still heaving from our workout, his eyes serious. "Then we talk."

I nod in agreement.

*Hoping like hell my words can be as convincing as everything I can say when we aren't talking. Everything makes more sense when I'm in his arms and his lips are against mine.*

# Nash

*WHY DO I keep doing this? What the hell is wrong with me?* It's like I lose all sense when I'm alone with him. I told Hayden I wasn't going to fuck him, and then the first thing I do is fuck him. Well fuck against him. His cock against mine with my hand wrapped around us together.

*Jesus Christ. I'm an idiot.*

There's no denying how good it felt. To touch him again. To kiss him again. To get lost in him. But that's the problem, isn't it? I let myself get way too lost in him once. I can't go through that again.

We silently clean up together in my bathroom, and I try not to notice the delicious pink hue to his cheeks as I use a washcloth to wipe away the evidence of our release and then zip my pants up. He's always that shade of pink after he comes.

*No. Stop thinking like that.*

He zips up too, and we toss the cloths in the hamper before I lead him back to the living room. We sit down on the couch, and I try to keep a safe distance before I ask, "What changed?" When he first got here, he was terrified of me outing him. Now all of a sudden, he's ready to be out? It just doesn't make sense.

"Nash." His eyes beg me to listen to him, and I do. "I don't know exactly. It just all snapped into place. You being here. Being near you again. Seeing Hayden. Seeing the sort of family you all have built. Samantha being so ambivalent about fucking other people because what we had was literally nothing. I knew I was living a lie, but maybe in the back of my mind, I'd convinced myself she was happy even if I knew it wasn't true."

"Look, Adrian, if you want to come out, that's great. But you can't do it for me or for anyone else. And if you want that, then you can't hide it. Not for anyone. That's a pain like none other."

He flinches. "I know, but I can do this for you."

"No," I say firmly. "You can't. Law and Rae, they'll figure something else out." My heart aches in my chest. It feels like someone has a fist wrapped around it, squeezing tight. "But if you're not ready to come out, then don't. Just don't."

"I want to," he says emphatically, and I believe him, but I'm not sure he's actually ready. "I really want to. I can't live like this anymore, Nash. You know what my life has been like the last few years?"

"No idea." Even though I've thought about him every single day since he left and wondered that very thing.

"I wake up. I go to the office. I put on my fake persona and smile for the cameras when needed. I meet Samantha when I'm supposed to, and then I go home to an empty house that's nothing like this." He looks around my cabin like it's something to behold, and then his eyes meet mine again. "It's professionally decorated because I didn't care enough about it to pick out things I liked. It's huge, way too big for only me. And it's quiet. So damn quiet that I have to turn on the television to try to drown out the loneliness as I sip my expensive scotch and then go to bed."

Honestly, that's pretty close to what I'd pictured. That's the other version of Adrian I knew. Sad and lonely. Doing his father's bidding and having no opinion of his own when he was around his parents. "That's sad."

"It is," he agrees emphatically. But then he smiles as he looks around my place again. "*This* is what I want."

I raise my hands, panicking because I can't let myself get lost. "Whoa. We just got each other off. We aren't building a life together or anything."

He frowns slightly at that, but then he laughs. And it's his real laugh. One I used to know so damn well. One I felt pride in every time

I made the sound come from his lips. "That's not what I meant." *Oh.* He shakes his head at me and laughs again, looking whimsical as he gazes out the window of the cabin. "I meant this life, where it's warm and comfortable. Where I have decent people around me, and it's also calm. Peaceful. Where people aren't expecting things from me that I can't deliver."

He looks more certain in this moment than I've ever seen him. "If that's what you want, then you should have it."

"That's what I want."

"But you can't pretend anymore, if you're really going to go for it. You can't be her bitch."

He winces, and I know I've struck a nerve. But I also know he needs to hear it. "I hurt you." His eyes meet mine, and I see the guilt swimming in them. "I hurt you badly. I can do this easily."

"Play her boyfriend during the day?"

He shrugs. "Pose for photos and go to events with her while we're here. Keep her happy until we check out, and this place is set for years instead of months. I want to do this, Nash. And I can."

I want to tell him it's stupid and he shouldn't, but I think about Rae and Law. How Samantha, whether I like her or not, has helped make good things happen for this place. "You shouldn't have to hide who you are. Rae and Law would be so pissed, knowing what she's doing to you."

He looks pained. "It's for the greater good though, right? For once in my life, I can actually do something good."

"What about your father?"

He rubs the back of his neck with his hand, and I know how tense his father makes him. "I guess I'll keep him happy until we're checked out of here too. But it won't be difficult. He barely checks in with me. I doubt I'll see him until then anyway." He moves a little closer to me and places a hand on my knee. "I'm sorry I hurt you, Nash. Let me do this. Something good."

He did hurt me. But I can see he hurt himself just as much. "Why?"

"Because I need to."

I shake my head. "No. I mean, why didn't you show up? I thought you would be there. I stood there for so long, waiting on you. I really thought you were going to show up, Adrian."

He looks defeated, removing his hand from my knee, his shoulders drooping. "I don't have a good reason for that."

"No good reason?" I stand up, annoyance flaring inside me. "How about *any* reason? Anything. Some sort of explanation of how we went from us running away together and planning to be together forever, to me finding out that you left for college on fucking Facebook. You couldn't even call me to tell me that you were ditching me, Adrian?"

He stands up too. "I couldn't."

"You couldn't?"

"I couldn't hear your voice, Nash. I knew . . ."

"What?" I move closer to him, glaring into his eyes, pleading with him for an answer to a question I've been asking for so long. "You. Knew. What?"

"That I wouldn't be able to leave you behind."

I toss my hands up in frustration and anger as I step back. "That's just fucking great." I start to walk away from him but then turn around, looking him dead in the eye because I need more. "Would that have been so bad? To actually go with me? To be with me?"

He shakes his head and opens his mouth to answer, but I hold up a hand to stop him.

"You know what? Don't answer that. Just get out. Leave. Because I don't want to know the answer. I let you break me once, but I'm not doing this again."

He starts toward me, but I keep up my defensive stance.

"Go."

He looks like a kicked puppy, and I hate that I did that to him, but this is all too much. With his head hung low, he takes a deep breath and exits my cabin.

*Good. It's better this way.*

*Just keep telling yourself that, Nash.*

# Nash

"OKAY, not that I don't love this whole grumpy-bear thing you've got going . . ." I glare at Hayden. But it's not him I'm mad at, and he knows it. He plops down next to me around the fire that's slowly dying out. "But you're going to have to talk to me."

"No."

He rolls his eyes at me. "Do we really have to play this whole game again where you tell me no, but then talk to me because I'm totally your best friend?"

I let a smile slip at that, and he grins because he knows, without a doubt, he's right. "It's nothing, Hayden. You already know what's bugging me."

His eyes flash over to the cabin Adrian is sharing with Samantha and then turns a sympathetic look back to me. I've avoided them both all day today after kicking Adrian out of my cabin last night. I couldn't face him, and I couldn't stand to see him playing her game. Thankfully, it's dark out now and late, so I'm banking on almost everyone being done for the night. "So, he's really with her, I'm guessing?"

"No." I lean back in my seat, letting my long legs stretch out. "He's not. Or at least he says he's not. But he knows if he pisses her off too much, she'll destroy this place, so he's playing her little games and hiding in the closet."

Hayden seems pensive for a moment and then stares absently at the flames of the fire. "So, he told her?"

"That he's gay?" He nods, and I look at the same fire he is. "He did. And apparently, she was terrible about it but still wants him to play her future-husband role."

"How terrible?"

I shrug. "I don't know. I didn't ask him for the details. He says he wants to be out, that he's ready for that. But how can he be when he's with her? And he's still willing to be with her, to let the world think he's hers."

I can tell he's deep in thought again even though I'm not looking at him directly. "It's kind of nice that he wants to help Rae and Law."

He turns his head to look at me, and I look at him. "They'd be pissed if they knew that's what he was doing just for them."

He smiles at that and doesn't disagree. "That they would, for damn sure. But I don't know, Nash. Not everything is so black and white. Seems to me, he's trying to make up for something bad."

"You really think it's okay to let him do that? To hide in the closet? To pretend to be someone he's not?"

He shrugs, but before he can answer, we're both startled by the cabin door opening and Adrian walking outside, his heavy black winter coat zipped up to his neck and a black beanie over his normally perfectly styled hair. He approaches us cautiously but with purpose and sits down next to Hayden.

Hayden stands. "I'll let you two talk."

"No," we both say, and Hayden stalls his movement, looking uncertain about what to do, although I'm sure he'd rather run.

"You should stay. You're Nash's friend, and I know you care about him," Adrian says quietly but firmly in Hayden's direction, and he carefully sits back in his seat. Adrian is still looking only at him. "He told you about Samantha?"

Hayden nods. "How you're going to play her doting fiancé for the greater good."

Adrian looks slightly taken aback, like he can't figure out if Hayden is fucking with him or not, and it's a good call because

Hayden is smart. No one really knows what he's thinking. "Ummm..."

Hayden doesn't make him finish. "You're going to let her play the perfect hetero couple and force yourself back deep in the closet to make sure Rae and Law get rave reviews on their place. And then what?"

Adrian holds his head up high, looking Hayden in the eye, unafraid and knowing he's being grilled right now. "I'm letting her use me for photo ops like she has for years until we check out. I'm not going back in the closet, Hayden. I won't." He glances my way briefly, but then he looks back to Hayden. "I've made it clear to her that I'm not with her and that I'm gay."

I can't fight the surprise every single time he says that. And the smile on his face when he does . . . I can't deny it does something to me. Hayden just nods his head, thinking something over. "And how did she take that?"

He winces, and goddammit, I'm feeling sorry for him again. "Not well. I didn't realize how truly vile she was." He grips the back of his neck, and I can feel the tension from here. "That's actually why I'm out here." He looks at the fire and not at either of us. "I was hoping there was somewhere else I could stay." His eyes meet mine. "I can't spend another night under the same roof as her."

"That bad, huh?" Hayden asks, but there's no malice in his tone. I can hear his sympathy.

Adrian's voice cracks only slightly as he nods. "Vile."

Hayden's hand moves to Adrian's shoulder, squeezing it. "No one should have to deal with something like that. I'm sorry." He sighs. "You can stay with me."

*Wait. What?* I don't even have a chance to really think about my reply, it's that immediate, and I let out a deep, low growl. "No."

Both of their gazes land on me. Hayden looks amused. And Adrian just looks defeated as he stands up, his shoulders slumping. "Okay."

I huff and stand up, looking at Adrian and ignoring Hayden's grin. "I mean, you can stay with me. You stayed in my cabin last night anyway. You're used to my couch."

*Lame. Totally lame.*

Thankfully, he doesn't call me on it. He just gives me a sweet, thankful smile. "Thank you. I appreciate it, Nash."

Hayden stands up, a big ole smile on his face. "That's really nice of you, Nash." He slaps my back, and I growl, but he only laughs. Then his expression turns serious as he embraces Adrian in a hug. His voice is quiet, but I still catch what he says, "You don't owe it to anyone to hide who you are because you're more than good enough, just the way you are."

Adrian looks frozen, his eyes watery when Hayden releases him and winks at me before walking away, leaving us alone.

"He's not wrong," I say, uncertain of exactly how to follow that.

Adrian swallows, opens his mouth but then shuts it again like he's too choked up to speak. And I get it. That's probably all he needed to hear his whole life. Maybe I didn't say it clearly enough when we were younger. Too lost in the moment with him. Enjoying being with him too much to stop and really talk about serious things.

"Come on." It's past dinner time, and we aren't having a bonfire tonight, so I quickly put the fire out and lead him back to my cabin. It's not too late, but he looks completely wiped out.

I close the door behind us and then turn back to tell him he's welcome to anything he needs here. But before I can get the words out, my lips are met with his. I should push him away and tell him it was only yesterday that I told him to go.

But I don't do that. His coat and hat are gone, and I dig my fingers through his mussed hair, clinging to him as I kiss him deeply.

*He's my weakness, and I'll regret it later. But for now, I'm going to be a little selfish and just give in.*

# Adrian

PLEASE DON'T STOP.

It's all I can think of as we kiss by the front door of Nash's cabin. *Please don't stop.*

I want this. I want him. More than I've ever wanted anything in my life. Even if it's only for a night. Even if he pushes me away again right after this. I just want him.

I need him.

His fingers grip my hair tighter, and I moan into his mouth, cherishing every minute of forbidden pleasure as he nips at my bottom lip and his larger body is pressed against mine. It's frantic and messy. Much like it always was with us before. We never had much time together, and it was like we couldn't ever get enough.

I unzip his coat and push it off his broad shoulders, not taking my mouth off his as I thrust my tongue inside to tangle with his. I hate having to break the kiss for even a second, but I need more skin. I move back only slightly to remove his t-shirt and toss it behind us, taking the moment to stare at his sculpted chest.

My hand brushes over the dusting of hair between his pecs and then slides down over his cut abs. "Jesus."

He grins, and then his lips are back on mine, pushing my body back toward the living area, and I go willingly, removing my own shirt as we go. I feel his hands roam over my back and then move to

129

my ass as he squeezes and pulls me into him. Our cocks are hard as they grind together through the fabric of our pants.

"More," I gasp desperately as he lifts me, my legs going around him momentarily before my back hits the couch and his body is blanketing mine, nearly knocking the wind out of me. But I grab the back of his neck and hold him to me as we continue to kiss.

*Please don't stop.*

My mind is a mess, but I know this is everything I want and need, so I don't allow even a second for either of us to think. I don't want to think. I just want to feel.

He starts to pull back, but I don't let him, biting his bottom lip and shaking my head when he tries to move away from my mouth. "Please." It's all I get out before his lips press harder against mine and we can barely catch our breath. He grinds against me, and I thrust upward, seeking friction and wanting so much more. "I want you inside me, Nash," I manage to say against his lips.

There's a sharp exhale from him, like he's surprised to hear it. His mouth withdraws, and his forehead rests against mine, like he's taking time to think about it. As much as I want it and as desperate as I am for him not to overthink it, I know I can't be that selfish. He should only do this if he wants me too.

"You're sure?"

I nod, the skin of our foreheads rubbing together before he sits up on his knees between my parted thighs.

*Please don't stop.*

He stands, and my heart pounds painfully in my chest as I fear him kicking me out again. But he doesn't. He pushes his pants down along with his black boxer briefs, leaving me breathless as I take in his naked form. He's solid muscle. Every bit of him is a work of sculpted art, including his cock that's standing proud and leaking at the tip. It's thick and long with prominent veins and even more glorious than I remembered it.

I'm staring, taking him in and unable to look away, but I don't apologize for it. If this is all I get, I'm going to soak it in. "You're beautiful, Nash."

He's confident and strong, exuding a fierce strength he's always had but has become more prominent as he's gotten older. As he kicks away his pants and briefs, he grabs my hand, pulling me off the couch. "Get naked."

I nod dumbly as he leaves the room, and my eyes stay fixed on his tight ass as he walks away, the muscles flexing with each stride.

Then his command registers, and I quickly push my pants and briefs off, leaving myself totally naked in the middle of his living room before he comes back. I smile when I see he has a condom and lube in his hand, my heart rate kicking up again, knowing I'm going to get what I so desperately need.

He nods toward the wall. "There."

I take the order, not used to being submissive, but for once, it's what I want too. My hand rests against the cool wall as my breathing increases and my nerves start to kick in. Not about the sex. I trust Nash. I don't know if that's stupid or not, but I've always trusted him

I know he won't intentionally hurt me, and honestly, I crave the burn. The slight bite of pain before the pleasure. The feeling of being alive again.

And when I sense his large body behind me, there's no fear, only relief. His hands smooth over my back and over the globes of my ass as his breath hits my neck. "You're the beautiful one, Adrian. You always have been."

When he says it, I believe him. "Please, Nash." I'm desperate, my voice almost a whine that makes him chuckle slightly.

"Patience."

I shake my head and rest my forehead against the wall. "None left."

His lips kiss against the side of my neck and then down my shoulder and back. He kneels behind me, and I feel his hands on my thighs, urging me to part them. I do what he wants without any hesitation. "Your ass has only gotten better."

He's still not touching me the way I want. The fucker is really going to tease the hell out of me this time, I can feel it. But I'll give him anything he wants. I stand still and feel his lips on my left cheek, leaving a soft kiss that's almost sweet. Then I feel his teeth dig in, and

I flinch and moan at the same time when he drags his tongue over the same spot, kissing it and soothing the slight ache.

"You're going to kill me, Nash."

"Nah, you'll live." He repeats the action on the other cheek, and I try like hell to remember to be patient as I spread my legs further, silently begging him to keep going. His tongue drags down my crack, and we both moan when he rims my hole.

He groans deeply, and it's almost as if he's enjoying it as much as I am. His tongue licks and probes, softening me to take his big cock. I'm dying for him to be inside me. His tongue feels incredible, but I need more as I hump against the wall, needy and aching. Wanting friction. "Please."

When he pulls away, I whimper embarrassingly loudly, and when I hear the cap of the lube bottle open, I nearly sob in relief. He starts with one finger, being gentle with me. But I don't want gentle. I move my hips back, fucking his finger and pleading for more. He grants my wish and adds another finger, but it's still not enough. "How long has it been since someone was inside you, Adrian?"

God, even his voice is sexy. Deep and low, full of rasp. "You." I can barely think as he sinks in further and hits my prostate, eliciting the whiniest, desperate moan from me. "You were the last one. The only one. Please, Nash."

I swear, I can feel his smile as he presses a kiss against my ass cheek and then adds more lube and another finger. "You want me again?"

"God, yes." I fuck backwards on his fingers. "I need more. I need your cock, Nash."

He adds another finger, stretching me for him. "Tell me how much."

"Ungh." I can't seem to form actual words, my cock leaking like crazy as I thrust, and my balls feel full and heavy, pleading for release. "More than I've ever wanted anything. Please, Nash. I need it. I need you. Now."

He removes his fingers. Not saying a word as he stands, and I hear him putting on the condom before I feel his hard cock pressing against my hole in a teasing manner but still not going inside.

"Nash."

His fingers grab my hair as he turns my head and presses his lips to mine in a bruising kiss as he slides into me too slowly. I want it all. I want it hard. I want to feel him for days. Weeks. I want to never forget this feeling.

I tilt my hips back, giving him a better angle as he slides into my body. "I won't break. Fuck me, Nash."

He growls, his teeth finding my neck as he nips and sucks and pushes into my body, his cock stretching me and leaving me with a full feeling and the delicious burn I crave.

"Yes." I push my hips back, silently begging him to move as he fully seats himself inside my ass. "Please."

His hand is still in my hair, gripping it hard, pulling my head back to feast on my neck, and I love it. I love every single moment of it. "You feel so fucking good. So tight around my cock."

"Yes," I pant. "Move, Nash. Fuck me. I can take it. I want it."

He obliges. Finally. He pulls back, leaving only the tip inside before thrusting forward in one strong, beautifully fluid motion, hitting me deep and pressing against my prostate and making me see stars. My fingers clench against the wall, trying to gain purchase as he thrusts inside me, and I move with him, begging for each punishing stroke.

He fucks into me with abandon as we both get lost in the moment. Our bodies are slick with sweat as we move together. "I'm close." *God, am I close.*

His teeth sink into my shoulder as he moves in and out, thrusting hard and deep, hitting the perfect spot every single time. My thighs are quaking, and I'm not sure I'll be able to stand up much longer. His big hand leaves my hair, and when it wraps around my cock, still slick from when he prepped me, I'm a fucking goner.

I thrust into his hand, relishing every second of his cock filling me up. With a harsh cry, I spill over his hand, a whimpering, needy mess. I feel his cock swell inside of me, jerking with his release as we both sag against the wall, me pressed between Nash's body and the wall.

*And then, I wait for the inevitable.*
*For him to tell me to leave and never come back.*

# Nash

WELL, that's not at all what I expected to happen. I want to say I'm an idiot and tell him it was a mistake, but I can't. I can barely move as my body presses against his. My dick is sated and has slipped from his body. I need to get rid of the condom, but I can't seem to move.

When we were kissing, I kept telling myself I needed to stop. But it was like I could hear him pleading with me not to. And I didn't want to. So, then I told myself I would fuck him fast and hard. Scratch the itch. But then, when he was there, naked, needy, and desperate for me, I couldn't do that either.

I took my time with him, but not nearly as much as I wanted to. I wanted to lay him on my bed and explore every inch of his body. Get reacquainted and notice all the changes too. He has more muscle than he once had, but he's still lean and compact.

"Shower?" I meant it to come out as a sharp command, but it's more of a vulnerable question. And that's exactly how I feel right now.

Stripped bare, inside and out.

He nods. I finally pull my body away from his, but his hand reaches out, his fingers sliding between mine. I look into his eyes, seeing he's feeling just as vulnerable as I am. I tighten our hold and pull him toward the bathroom.

I turn on the shower and dispose of the condom as I watch him climb in and go under the spray. He lets the water fall over his face, and I stare in awe of him. I wasn't lying when I said he's the beautiful one. His lithe, lean muscles are flexed tight now but relax under the water. His ass is biteable and firm. So fucking sexy as water slides over his sculpted mounds. He's absolute perfection.

I climb into the glass shower, pulling the door closed. He turns around to face me, the water running down his back, but the droplets slide down his face. His hazel eyes bore into me, waiting for me to say something, but I can't come up with any words.

Instead, my hands move to his flat stomach, defined but not as cut as my own. His skin is soft as I rest my palm over it, and he sucks in a sharp inhale of air. "I'm sorry."

I don't ask why he's apologizing. I can guess, but I don't want to talk right now. I grasp the back of his neck and pull his lips to mine, kissing him as we slide under the showerhead, the water raining down on us through our kiss.

His hands hold onto my hips, and I can feel myself growing hard again against him. I feel his cock hardening too, our kiss deepening, but neither of us move to do more. Our lips and tongues do all the talking we need to right now as we allow the shower to soak us, neither of us in a hurry.

When I pull away, it's only to grab the body wash and pour it into my hand before I soap up his body. He does the same for me. We both take our time. My hands roaming all over him, every dip every hardened muscle. I'm careful when I move between his legs, ignoring his dick that's rock hard now and moved to his used hole. I'm gentle, knowing he has to be sore.

*Only me.*

I'm the only one who's been inside him. It's a heady feeling, my chest filling with pride when he acknowledged that. All I wanted to do was take care of him in that moment. I just wanted him to feel good, to feel me.

His soapy hand wraps around my aching dick, and I groan, pulled from my thoughts at the feeling of him gripping me tight and stroking. My forehead rests against his as my hand finally acknowledges his dick, wrapping around it and finding the same rhythm.

We kiss as we thrust into each other's hands slowly, taking our time with each other. He's the first to lose himself to pleasure, his cum spilling over my hand before my balls draw up tight and I come, my toes trying to dig into the tile of the shower floor.

We don't talk as we rinse off, climb out, and then dry off. We still don't say anything as we make our way to my bedroom and I hand him sweats and a shirt to wear. We dress, and I sit on the edge of the bed.

It's been so long since I've allowed another person to get close to me. Since I've cared enough to talk about anything from the past. But I have to know. I can't take it anymore. "Why?" He also moves to sit on the bed but keeps space between us as our eyes meet. "Why didn't you show up that night? I waited. I thought you'd be there."

"I wanted to be."

"What happened?" I keep my voice calm, even though I feel anything but that.

To his credit, he doesn't look away from me. He doesn't run. "No explanation will make it acceptable. You know that. I know that. It was horrific what I did."

"It doesn't matter. I just want to know." My voice raises slightly now. "You owe me that."

He looks defeated. His shoulders slump as he seems to accept that. He looks broken as his eyes stay firmly on mine. "I'm a coward. A total coward."

"That's not good enough, Adrian. We had plans. We . . ." I stand up, the emotions surging through me are too painful. I look back at him, "We were going to make a life together. We were young, but I wasn't imagining how much we cared about each other, was I?"

He stands too, walking closer to me, but leaving a few inches between us. "No." His gaze is fierce. "You didn't imagine that. I loved you more than I'd ever loved anyone or anything."

"Then why?" I barely choke the words out, but I manage.

He closes the gap, his hand resting on my shoulder as his eyes bore into mine. "I was no one. I was a shell of a human, groomed for one thing and one thing only." I watch his throat flex and pull tight, the veins becoming more prominent. "My father's trained bitch boy. I did what he said. I was told what to wear. Where to go. When to be there. And I did it. Until you, I followed their path."

"So why didn't you go with me? You hated that."

"I did," he agrees, and he seems laser-focused in this moment, determined to have me hear him. And I'm listening.

"So. Why?"

"I'm telling you. I had nothing to offer, Nash."

"That's bullshit." I walk away from him, yanking away from his hold. Furious at him. At his parents. At everyone who told him he wasn't good enough. I turn to face him, fury slicing through me. "You had *you* to offer. That's all I ever wanted, Adrian. You."

He looks pained as he takes a deep breath and then a step in my direction. "But I had no skills. None. I was born with a silver spoon in my mouth and had zero survival skills. What was I going to do to help support us? Without college?"

I open my mouth for a moment and then close it again. We'd discussed getting jobs. I had some experience in construction on the weekends and figured I could find a job like that wherever we went. But I hadn't really thought about what he would have done. "I would have taken care of you."

"Exactly!" He raises his hands in the air as if there's some big epiphany I should be having.

"What? What the hell is wrong with me taking care of you? Would that have been so goddamn bad?"

"Yes." I flinch, and he takes another step forward, his hand brushing over my cheek. "Nash, look at me."

I didn't realize I'd looked away, but I meet his eyes slowly. "You didn't want to be with me?"

He shakes his head, a small smile forming on his lips. "Nash, that's all I ever wanted, but I didn't want you taking care of me. I wanted to be your partner. Someone you could depend on. And I chickened out."

"We would have figured it out."

"How?" He looks so damn crushed. "You would have been so damn busy, trying to keep me safe and fed, and I had nothing to offer you. Nothing. I had no skills. No survival instincts. I would have held you back, and you would have done everything you could to keep us both going. We would have drowned, Nash."

"You don't know that."

"I do."

I move into him, our chests touching now. "You don't. You didn't give us that chance. We could have made it. Together. We could have come out stronger than before, but you robbed us of that."

"Or we could have been worse. You could have ended up trying to save me, and we both would have failed. It's what you do, Nash. You rescue."

"We would have had each other. We would have been okay as long as we had each other. I could have taught you. You weren't nothing, Adrian. You were my fucking everything."

His forehead rests against mine as a quiet sob escapes his throat. "I didn't know. I was scared. I didn't know what life with you could be like." His breath moves over my lips. "I've only had a small taste since I've been here, and I'm so sorry. God, Nash, I'm so sorry."

I pull back, gripping his face in my hands, and I press a kiss to his forehead. "I'm sorry too. I should have talked to you more. I knew you were nervous, and I should have gone deeper into it. I was just so damn excited about starting a life with you, I didn't think about the things you'd be giving up."

His eyes snap up to mine. "I would have given it all up gladly. I didn't want that life then either. I swear it. I just didn't want to hold you back. I couldn't stand for my favorite person in the world to end up hating me and thinking I was worthless too."

"You are not worthless. You've never been worthless." I look straight into his eyes that are shining with unshed tears.

"I want this." It's a quiet whisper. "I know you don't trust me. But I want this so badly."

"I can't ever hide who I am again, Adrian. Not even for you."

139

"I know." He presses his lips against mine softly. "Can we just take it slow? Maybe give it a chance?"

My heart clenches tightly in my chest as I look into those hazels that have haunted me for so long, and I know I can't say no to him. "Okay."

*Stupid, dumbass heart.*

# Adrian

*TAKING IT SLOW.*

That's what we agreed to a few days ago. I lie on my side and take in Nash's naked form, drinking in every cut muscle. Every scar. Every single detail.

The sun is starting to rise in the sky. It's snowed a lot over the past two days, so that's pretty much all I can see as I look out the window of his bedroom. But as the sun streams into his room, it catches his beautiful face, illuminating him. The man I've missed so damn much and tried hard to never allow myself to think about.

He's here. Asleep and naked right next to me. His thick beard can't hide his sharp cheekbones and gorgeous face. He looks peaceful as I drag my finger through his soft beard and over his bottom lip.

I haven't been around Samantha much at all lately, and it's been great. Instead, I've mostly been spending time with Nash and Hayden. Going for walks in the woods around the lake. Hell, even chopping firewood with them. And I've learned quickly.

Which only helps solidify what an idiot I was when I left him behind. Maybe we could have made it out on our own, just the two of us. Maybe he could have taught me, and we would have survived. I could have had this life.

"You're thinking pretty hard." Nash's voice is a sexy, sleepy rasp as his lips turn up into a beautiful smile.

"I'm an idiot," I blurt, and his eyes open with a questioning glance.

"Why?"

"I could have learned to work in construction or hell, even fast food. I could have, and I should have done that for you."

He looks sympathetic as his hand finds the side of my head, and he pulls me to him for a kiss. It's brief, and I groan in protest when he pulls back to look me in the eye. "We don't get to change the past. You weren't ready then."

"I'm an idiot."

He laughs at that, and the full-bodied laugh that falls from his mouth is intoxicating. "You're not." His large shoulder shrugs upward. "Or at least I hope not anymore."

I shake my head adamantly. "I want this, Nash."

He still looks uncertain. And honestly, who could blame him after what I did? "How is this going to work? You're still . . ." He looks like he's trying to put it delicately, and I hate it. I don't want to be treated like I'll break. I want him to get mad at me. To tell me what he's thinking, no matter what.

"I'm still what?" I rest my head on my hand as I prop myself up on my elbow, facing him.

He looks away from me, his face showing the haunts of pain I've caused. "You're still hers."

"No." I reach out my free hand and rest it over his rapidly beating heart. "I'm not. I never was."

He turns to face me now, laying on his side but allowing my hand to stay on his heart. "You can't keep doing this for her. She doesn't deserve it." His hand traces over my cheek and then rests there. "She doesn't deserve you."

I internally fight the need to argue with him. To tell him I'm not so great. Not even close. "She doesn't have me. She has the online persona. An illusion."

"I don't want her to even have that."

I don't either. I cringe every time she posts something about us being a happy couple. Or about our future. "I want so much for your family. I want Rae and Lawson to have this. They deserve it."

"I need to tell them."

I'm careful with my question. "Tell them what?"

"About what she's doing. About who she really is." We talked in-depth about the conversations I've had with her since I told her I was gay. And about her family's views and mine. About the post with the gay couple in the background being taken down. About every disgusting act.

I breathe in slowly and close my eyes, letting myself feel his heartbeat.

"Adrian. I won't tell them if you're not ready for everyone to know about—"

My eyes open and smile. "Me being gay?"

He nods. "I'll never out you. And neither will Hayden." He shrugs. "Even though Lawson pretty much knows too."

I smile bigger. "I like that." He looks surprised as I lay a kiss on his lips and breathe him in, resting my forehead against his. "I love being out and open with who I am. I'm not worried about that."

"You aren't?" He sounds unsure, and I get it. I was so adamant at first that he not tell anyone about us but then the dam broke, and everyone important to him figured it out, and it just wasn't so scary anymore.

"I'm not. I just don't want your brother and Rae to suffer."

"She's not that powerful. The good have to win over the hate, Adrian. They have to. And it will kill them to know that someone like that helped progress the success of their business. This place is their life."

I nod my head and kiss him again. "I understand. You do whatever you need to do. I'm behind you, and I'll do whatever I can to keep it as drama-free as possible. But Samantha is cunning, and I'm afraid she'll be vindictive."

"I'm not afraid of her. But I am a little scared of Rae." I chuckle, and he pushes me onto my back, his larger body holding me down, and it feels way too good. "You laugh, but that tiny human is fucking fierce when she's mad. And she'll be pissed when she finds out what a cunt your future fiancé is."

I laugh, no part of me wanting to defend Samantha. My hands

move down his back and rest over his ass. "Not *my* future." I look into his eyes, hopefully portraying that Samantha is not my future. That I hope *he* is. "I believe you. And you never, ever have to hide anything from anyone because of me. Never again."

I see the happiness swimming in his eyes as he dips down to kiss me deeply this time, his hardening cock grinding against mine.

"That gets you excited, huh?"

His mouth moves over my jaw and down to my neck where he nips and bites, soothing the sting with kisses. "I'm pretty sure everything about you gets me excited."

I laugh just as my phone pings on the nightstand next to the bed. His lips move back to mine as he kisses me and then breathes against my lips, "Do you need to get that?"

"Fuck, no." I thrust upward, letting his cock glide against mine and throw my head back in pure ecstasy.

"It could be important."

"No more talking, Nash." I kiss him hard, and our bodies move together as we take our time, relearning every single piece of one another, and when he finds a condom, rolling it on and then slides inside me again, I know, without a doubt, this is where I'm supposed to be.

*I'll do anything I can to keep him this time.*

*No more being a coward.*

# *Nash*

TURNS out the message Adrian ignored was from his father, letting Adrian know he'll be here next week for Thanksgiving. He didn't say anything after that, but I know he's nervous. How could he not be?

Still, after a shower, we're dressed and are heading to Lawson and Rae's cabin. I don't know how to label what we are at the moment, whether we're together or not. But when we walk inside and Adrian takes my hand in his, it sure feels like we're together.

I'd be lying if I said I didn't love that thought.

Rae and Law eye our hands, both with grins on their faces, but neither say anything. Hayden is here too, sitting on their couch, flipping through channels on the television. When he turns to look at us, a knowing smirk spreads over his beautiful face. "Aw, did you two finally get your shit together? How cute."

I use my middle finger to scratch my nose, effectively giving him the finger, and he only laughs. Raelynn looks slightly lost, but I know she's already figured out a lot on her own, even if Lawson didn't tell her everything. If he did, I wouldn't be upset. She's his wife.

"Okay, so what's happening here?" Rae asks as she sits next to Hayden on the couch. "You two are together now?"

Adrian clenches my hand a little tighter, like he's afraid I'm going to pull away. I don't want to hurt him, but I want to protect myself too. "We're figuring it out," I say vaguely and direct Adrian to the living room with me, both of us sitting in the oversized chair next to the couch.

Lawson takes a seat next to Rae, wrapping his arm around her shoulders. "Figuring it out? And what does your girlfriend think about that?" He directs his question at Adrian.

Who squirms in his seat. "She's not my girlfriend. I ended things with her a few days ago."

They all look skeptical, and who could blame them? Hayden picks up his phone but doesn't bother unlocking the screen. "Social media says otherwise."

I decide to take over now. "That's kind of why we're here."

Rae looks concerned, her pretty eyes on me. "What's going on?"

Adrian surprises me, taking the lead yet again. "I'm gay. And I've been hiding that fact for a really long time. My family isn't exactly . . ." he pauses, searching for the correct word, "understanding."

"Bigoted assholes?" Hayden supplies, and Adrian actually smiles at that.

"Yeah."

Rae's expression turns sympathetic. "That's awful. I'm so sorry. Have you tried to tell them before?"

He shakes his head. "No. It was pretty much instilled in me from a young age that would never be okay. That I was to grow up, go to college, work for my father, and get married to a woman they approved of. And of course, have lots of kids."

Rae looks disgusted by that, and hearing the plan for his life makes my stomach roll too. "We met in high school. And fell pretty hard."

"And I fucked it up." Adrian looks pained, and I want to reach out for him but decide to comfort him later.

"And then Adrian showed up here, of all the places in the world?" I recognize that dreamy tone from my brother. He's a pretty big believer in fate.

We both nod. "He did." I try to address them all, not sure what the outcome will be after this conversation, but I know it's important to have. "And she was awful to him when he told her the truth." Adrian seems to shrink in his seat, and I'm sure he's thinking about that moment.

"How awful?" Rae's eyes are on Adrian.

"Pretty bad. She's pissed that I lied, and she should be. I shouldn't have used her that way."

"It seems to me like she's using you just as much. I mean," Rae lets out a frustrated puff of air and then continues, "I didn't know you were interested in men, but I didn't exactly believe all the bullshit posts on social media, especially after seeing you two together in person. It seems, though, her followers eat it up."

"They do. I've been the perfect, doting boyfriend for three years. But I never told her I was gay before or that I didn't really love her."

"And you think she's in love with you?" Rae sounds like she already knows the answer.

"I don't think she actually believes in love. It's just a means to an end. What we were supposed to do. Samantha and I, we're cut from the same cloth." His eyes drift to me. "I didn't think I would ever have actual love."

I smile at him and then look away, trying to fight the fuzzy feeling deep in my gut, hearing him talk about love. Rae is grinning when my eyes meet hers. Then she turns back to Adrian. "So, she didn't know you were gay? You guys didn't have an arrangement before you got here?"

"No. She had no clue, and I'm sure she's blindsided." Adrian swallows hard, looking miserable. "But I didn't think she would be like that. Ever."

Hayden and I share a look, both wincing at the obvious residual pain he has from the things she's said to him. I place my hand on his shoulder and squeeze. "She had no right to treat you like that. None."

Rae stands up, determined. "Well, she has to leave. That's all there is to it. I want that hateful bitch out of here."

And this is where I figured it would go. "Rae . . ." I'm cautious.

Adrian cuts me off. "If you tell her to leave, she'll do everything she can to destroy the image of this place. I don't know what she'd do or the lies she'd tell, but her followers, they believe her. They trust her. It could hurt your business."

"And having someone like her recruiting other assholes to stay here is better for this place?" Yup, Rae is fired up, and she doesn't even know all the details. "No. This is not happening."

"Rae, maybe we need to think about this," Lawson says, reaching for her hand.

"No." She looks over at Adrian. "This is a place of love and acceptance. A safe space for anyone who needs it."

Raelynn survived an abusive stepfather. A man who thought he was above the law because in our small town, he was. I know how important it is that her part of the world is safe. "But what if there is no place after she's done?"

She stands up even straighter, her chin up. "Then there's not. But I . . ." She turns to Lawson. "We can't have that kind of people here." She sits down on the couch again, her back still deadly straight. "I knew who she was when she booked this place, but I thought she seemed kind. Just a traveler who happened to be a senator's daughter. And maybe I turned a blind eye to things I shouldn't have, but now, knowing she's full of hate?" Her gaze moves to me. "I can't allow that. I can't. She needs to leave, no matter what damage she leaves in her wake."

"Raelynn." We all turn to Adrian. "I can do this. She wants me to play the doting boyfriend a little longer, and then she'll leave, giving this place a glowing review, gaining who knows how many bookings for it."

"But at what cost? I don't want this place built on hate."

"She's more selfish than hateful. And for whatever reason, she needs her dad's approval above all else. But she's never said anything before this."

Hayden, who has been surprisingly quiet, speaks up now. "It doesn't matter, Adrian. The way she treated you? The way she's using blackmail to keep you in the closet and keep you from being the real you? That's not okay."

Adrian hangs his head, and I know none of this is easy for him. I squeeze his shoulder again, wanting to pull him to me. "You can't do this for her. We can't let you do that."

He nods his head slowly and looks directly at Rae as he stands up. "Okay. We'll leave. I'll tell her today the deal's off and that we need to leave."

My gut clenches tight at the thought of him leaving, but before I can say anything, Rae speaks up, "Not you. You should definitely stay."

Adrian looks surprised. "W-what? You know I'm from the same type of family she is, right?"

Rae smiles and stands, walking to him and taking his hand in both of hers. "It doesn't matter where you come from, Adrian. Believe me when I tell you that. I should know. My family is appalling, but it isn't an excuse to be a horrible person. And as far as I can tell, you're not."

"He's not," I speak up and stand next to him, our shoulders touching.

Rae grins at me, practically beaming. "Yeah. If Nash vouches for you, I believe him. And I haven't seen him smile—"

I interrupt, "I smile."

She's still beaming. "Not like this."

"Face it, you're normally a grumpy bastard." Lawson wraps his arm around my neck."

I roll my eyes, and Hayden stands too. "I happen to like his grumpy, growly self, but even I can't deny it's been nice to see him all chipper." He turns to Adrian. "You must be really, really good."

He winks, and I swear Adrian blushes.

"Okay, before we start with the group hugs and singing or some bullshit, I think we're gonna go," I say, but inside I can't deny how happy it makes me to see the most important people in my life standing together on this.

*And yeah, Adrian is included in that.*

# *Adrian*

*How the hell can they accept me?* They all look so happy, joking and laughing, but I'm barely holding it together. I'm grateful when Nash directs me out of Rae and Lawson's cabin and the door closes behind me.

It's all I can do not to drop to my knees in the cold snow because they're shaking so badly.

"Adrian?" Nash's concerned tone directs me to him. "Are you okay?"

"They want me to stay."

He nods, even though it wasn't a question. "They do. But they don't want her to."

"And if she destroys them? Everything you all worked for? How can they be okay with that?"

I know the answer already. *Integrity.* They're just plain good people. Nash places a hand on my shoulder. "Adrian, it's going to be okay."

"It's not though. How can they stand me? This is all my fault. All of it."

"What are you talking about?" He looks sincerely confused, and I should feel like an idiot. I'm about to have a breakdown in the middle of the cabin grounds as it starts to snow again. Big fat snowflakes hit my cold nose, but I can't move.

"All of it, Nash. I set all this in motion when I didn't show up at the lake house. When I left you behind and then got into a relationship that was more of a business arrangement my father set up. We came here, and now your life could potentially be wrecked because of me again."

His gloved hands cup my face as he jerks my attention to him. "This is not your fault, and we don't know what's going to happen yet. We have no idea, and I'm okay with that. You know why?"

I shake my head, still encased by his big hands. "Because I have you, goddammit. Or I hope I do."

"You do." I'm adamant. "But that can't be enough. Eventually you'll resent me."

"That's why you left me in the first place, remember? You don't get to decide our fate based on what could happen. You have to trust me, and I have to trust you, and that's all there is to it. Trust, Adrian."

His eyes are intense, burning into me as I pull cold air into my lungs and say, "I trust you."

He nods. "I trust you." I try to shake my head and tell him that he shouldn't, but he holds me firmly in place. "I trust you," he repeats.

"Why?" I choke out but just barely.

And he smiles. *Damn him.* He actually smiles. Big and bright. Sure. "You know why."

I grab his wrist, my hand wrapping around it. And I do. Even if he can't say the words again yet. Even if I don't deserve to hear them or I can't really get them to come out of my mouth again yet either. Not until I've earned it. "I want to tell her to pack her shit and get out. If that's what Raelynn and Lawson really want."

"Okay."

"But are you sure? One hundred percent sure that you don't care about the consequences? That they won't? Because I will gladly pay my dues to be around here. To be a part of all this, Nash. *Gladly.*"

He smiles, and then his cold lips press against mine. I smile as he kisses me sweetly but firmly out in the open in the broad daylight. I grip his coat and pull him even further into me, deepening the kiss and feeling more complete than I have in my entire life.

It feels like a beginning. A true beginning. Righting all the wrongs from my past. And when I hear the screech of my former girlfriend next to me, I don't fear anything. I don't pull away right away either. I only smile against Nash's mouth and then give him a quick peck before turning to an angry and semi-shocked Samantha.

"Adrian Walker, what the hell are you doing?" She keeps her voice low as her eyes dart around. No one else is outside at the moment, but she still looks frightened.

"Samantha, you need to leave."

"What?" She looks taken aback, her small glove-covered hand covering her heart. "What are you talking about?"

"I'm talking about you getting your things and leaving. Today. They don't want you here anymore. And neither do I."

Her eyes widen and they dart to Nash. "He's who you're fucking? *Him?*" She gestures wildly to Nash. "He doesn't even look gay."

Nash scoffs but doesn't say anything. "Jesus Christ." I pinch the bridge of my nose. "That's incredibly ignorant. And don't worry about Nash or anything here, just leave."

"I'm not leaving. You're making a scene, Adrian." She tries to grab at my hand, but I pull it away. "Come inside and talk to me. We have things to discuss."

"No."

Hayden, Rae, and Law must have heard the commotion because they all come out in full winter gear. Rae looks Samantha over and stands her ground. "You need to leave."

"Why?" Samantha looks truly puzzled. "Because my boyfriend decided all of a sudden he's into men and broke up with me?"

She really does play the victim well. Rae isn't having it though. "No. You need to leave because this is a safe place. This is an inclusive, loving place, and any type of hatred will not be tolerated."

Samantha huffs, placing her hands on her hips. "I don't hate gay people. I just didn't want my boyfriend to be gay."

"Well, he is. And instead of trying to understand that and accept him for him, you made him lie to the world. You threatened him with not fitting into your perfectly wrapped little box of bullshit. And that's not okay."

Samantha's bottom lip quivers, and I wish I felt sorry for her. I wish it was real, but I know her well enough to know it's not. "I'll ruin you. I'll go live and tell everyone to cancel their reservations. That I was treated horribly and told to leave for no reason."

Rae doesn't falter. Lawson wraps his arm around her small shoulders, and she stands tall. "You do what you have to do."

I don't want that though. I want them to thrive. They deserve only good things. Samantha's eyes zone in on me. "Is everyone here gay? Is that why you wanted to come here? To humiliate me?"

"Okay. You need to go now." Lawson's voice is calm but firm.

I don't point out that I had absolutely nothing to do with picking the venue. "You should go. Take everyone with you."

"Fine." She crosses her arms and makes no attempt to move. "But what about your father? Does he know yet?"

I feel Nash stiffen next to me. "Outing someone is just about the nastiest thing you can do."

"Fucking vile," Hayden adds.

But I don't care. "I plan to tell him very soon." I step closer to her. "And I plan to do it in person, so I can see his face when I do."

She looks shocked, searching my eyes and dropping her hands to her side. I see the instant she decides to switch tactics. She brings a hand up to cup my cheek, and again, I pull away from her. "Adrian, you can't do this. We need each other."

"I don't need you." Her hand falls away, and I step back. "And you know what?" I smile as I look around the beautiful backdrop of snow-covered cabins and pine trees. White fluffy snow coating the ground around us, and then my eyes narrow in her direction. "You can spread your bullshit lies, but if you do that, I'll repay the favor."

Her jaw drops slightly. "What are you talking about?"

"I have a pretty good following myself, thanks to you and you making me set up my accounts. And not to mention, I'm a prominent senator's son. If I really want to make a huge deal about this—about a popular travel blogger leaving a resort simply because she couldn't stand how many gay people were here—I fucking will."

I swear she gulps, and her eyes widen. "You wouldn't dare. You hate attention, Adrian."

I take a step closer to her, glaring and making sure my words hit home. "Try. Me."

I see Hayden smile brightly in my direction, but I keep my eyes on Samantha. "That would mean the whole world would know your dirty little secret, Adrian."

"It's none of those things, Samantha. I'm proudly gay. And it took me way too long to say it, but now that I have, I'm never going back to hiding anything about myself. These are good people who've been through hell. They deserve all the best, and you're going to give it to them, or I will ruin you and everything you care about."

I can feel Nash's shock as he stands next to me, and to be honest, I feel it too. The last thing I want is any attention on me, but I'll do it for him. I'm not bluffing.

"You can't do this." Her voice is high-pitched and whiny, but I don't flinch.

"I can, and I will. Or you can choose to be a decent human being and make up some excuse to why you had to leave. But let them know just how great this place is when you do."

I know Rae won't be thrilled about that part, but at the end of the day, as long as she leaves, I can't see the harm in her leaving on a positive note. She's already been raving about this place for weeks.

"I can't believe you, Adrian. Did you hit your head or something?"

"No. But this place is the first one that's made me feel sane in a long, long time. I love it here, and I'll be sure to say that repeatedly."

"You're making a huge mistake," she looks in Nash's direction and then back to me to sneer, "for him."

"He's everything, and anything but a mistake. Now. Go."

She looks like she wants to say something, but instead, she turns on her heeled boots and goes into her cabin. I sink into Nash's side as he wraps his arm around me and kisses the top of my head. "It's going to be okay."

*For the first time in a long time, I believe that too.*

# Nash

I GAVE the rest of the afternoon to Adrian, letting him rest at my place while I helped with stuff for the cabins. But I'm itching to get back to him. That couldn't have been easy, standing up to Samantha like that. Hell, it couldn't have been easy talking about it with Hayden, Rae, and Law either.

The day had to be draining for him.

When I walk into my cabin, I see him sitting on the edge of my bed in my room and make my way to him. "Hey."

He offers me a small smile, but I can see he's weary. His hair is still perfectly styled, and he's dressed in my clothes—sweats and a t-shirt that are too big for him. He said he couldn't bear to put on his old clothes, that they felt all wrong.

I know he's struggling.

"Hi."

I slip my coat off and put it on the chair next to my bed. I see his phone next to him. "You okay?"

His eyes move to the phone and then back to me as he nods slowly. "Yeah. My mom called to ask me what happened. I told her Samantha and I broke up, and she said she was very disappointed. But she didn't ask me why. She's going home too." He laughs, but it doesn't seem genuine. "I'm sure she couldn't wait to get out of here."

I sit next to him and pull him to me, letting his head rest on my shoulder. "They're gone. I saw their cars pull out of here an hour ago."

He nods, seeming nearly numb, and I wonder if I pushed him to this point too fast. I tried to tell him to slow down, but I also said I wouldn't hide ever again. "I'm glad they're gone."

"No one expects you to go on talk shows or anything, Adrian. Or to even post about your time here. Don't worry."

He lifts his head, his expression serious. "I'm not worried about having to do that, and I will if it comes to it. But I don't think she's going to do anything. Hopefully, I scared her just enough into being decent."

I nod cautiously. "What's the matter?"

He smiles, and this one seems real. "Nothing. I'm just processing. I'm kind of in awe."

"Me too." My body is tense when I ask, "Do you regret it?"

"No," he answers instantly. "Not at all. I just . . ." He turns his body more so he's facing me, and I do the same. "It was like I was drowning just underneath the surface for so long. And then you reached your hand down and grabbed me, pulling me up when no one else around me even noticed I was sinking. You pulled me out of it, and now I feel like the air has come back into my lungs and I'm alive. And it's a lot to process. I want to do so many things."

"Like what?"

He smiles again, brighter this time. "I want to tell my father before Samantha does."

"Are you sure that's not too fast for you?" I have to ask. I'm happy as hell to see the real Adrian again, and not only that, but also to see him set free. But it's a lot. He's not wrong.

But he looks slightly taken aback by my question and maybe even hurt. "You don't want me to?"

I flatten my hand over his smooth cheek. "I mean is it too fast for you? I just want to make sure it's not going to overwhelm you. It can wait. Hell, I get why you'd be nervous to tell him, Adrian."

"I want this, Nash." His hand covers mine. "I'm all-in. And I meant what I told Samantha. I want to see his face when I do it."

I believe him. There's something in his gaze that tells me all I need to know. He truly wants this. "I'll go with you."

He looks nervous now. "It won't go over well at all. Worse than Samantha. He'll be cruel, Nash, and I don't want him to hurt you."

I lean in, kissing his soft lips briefly and pull back only slightly. "I'm all-in too. I want to be there."

His eyes light up at that, and he nods his head in answer before his hands move to my chest and he pushes me back on the bed. "There are a lot of other things I want too."

I quirk a playful eyebrow because I like the lilt his voice has taken as he straddles me. "Oh yeah? And what could those *things* be?"

His hands move to the hem of my shirt, and he pulls it up slowly, teasingly. Only a sliver of skin is showing, and he drags his fingers over it. "So many things." He pulls it up a little more and leans forward, leaving brief kisses over my lower stomach. "You're so damn perfect, Nash."

I snort, "I'm anything but perfect."

He lifts the shirt further, his mouth latching onto my nipple and eliciting a loud, hungry moan from me before moving to the other. "You *are* perfect." He pulls on the shirt, and I lift up, assisting with the removal before he tosses it behind us. "I never thought I'd be here with you like this ever again."

I lift his shirt too, and we toss it away. I let my hands roam over his smooth, warm skin, completely in awe of him. I've only been with women since him, and while I can enjoy and appreciate curves, it's his hard lines and firm body that really gets me going. Maybe it's just Adrian himself. "I didn't think we'd ever be together again either. But I couldn't stop thinking about it."

His eyes roam over my chest and then to my face, his hands moving over my bare skin, but it's not enough. I want so much with him. I want everything. "I couldn't either. I thought about you every single day. And I would try to push it away." He leans forward, rolling his hips when he leans in to kiss me. We're both hard, and the fabric between us is frustrating as hell. "But I couldn't."

I thrust upward, letting my hips roll with his in a perfect, albeit slow, grind of our hard bodies against each other. And I kiss him harder because I couldn't either. His hands grab mine, pinning them to the side as we move together, both of us a panting mess. "Adrian," I say against his lips when we both come up briefly for air.

"I want you inside me again and again. I can't get enough of you, Nash."

I stay pinned beneath him, his hands holding mine, our fingers intertwined. "I want that too. I want you every way I can have you."

"You have me, for sure." He kisses my lips briefly and then releases me. He stands and strips as I kick away my jeans and briefs with lightning speed. He chuckles at my impatience, but I'm too far gone from wanting him.

He grabs a condom and lube from the drawer next to my bed and tosses them next to me on the bed. We've had the talk about him being tested after he found out Samantha and he were in an open relationship he had no idea about and that I've been tested since my last hookup that was ages ago. Still, that's as far as the conversation went.

I want to feel him bare, but part of me holds back. I don't know why. But when he straddles me, facing away and offers me his ass, I couldn't give a fuck about any thought in my head before that because, damn. "Jesus. You're the perfect one."

He chuckles at that but doesn't say anything. Instead, he just leans forward and swallows my dick. And I mean I feel the back of his throat and hear a gagging noise that makes my balls tingle, way too fucking close to a release.

"Fuck." He pulls back and then bobs his head again and again on my dick, and I'm afraid for a moment that this is going to be over before it starts. "Adrian, I don't want to come yet."

He pulls back, licking up my shaft and then saying, "Get me ready for this big cock, Nash, and I'll go slower."

I smirk and reach forward, gripping the firm globes of his ass in my hands and spreading them, groaning at the sight. I try to keep it together as he teases me, and I lean forward, letting my tongue circle his puckered hole. He moans around me, and I dig in, using my tongue and a finger to get him ready, already dying to be inside of him. I grab the lube, getting him slick and ready, stretching him with two fingers and then three before he begs me to get inside him.

He sheathes my cock with a condom and moves forward, positioning my cock at his slick hole. "I only want you, Nash. I want this."

I enter him at the agonizingly slow pace he sets, lowering himself over me. My hands grip his hip as I bottom out inside him, both of us groaning and grunting in ways that shouldn't be sexy but are so feral, I'm losing my mind.

I'm so far gone for him. He moves me in and out, but I can't take it. "I want to see your face, Adrian."

When he moves so my dick is no longer inside of him, my entire body begs for him to come back, but he only turns around and his warm, soft lips are on mine. His tongue teases mine as our cocks slide against each other. "I'm already so close."

I grab my cock, and he moves backward, placing me back in position to be inside him. When I thrust up and he moves down, my eyes close tight as I lose myself to pure pleasure. I grab his ass cheeks and let him ride me as we kiss and cling onto each other. "So good."

He nibbles on my bottom lip, breathless. "So fucking good."

His cock is slick with precum and lube from our grinding and being trapped between our bodies, and when I feel the sticky heat of his come splash over my abs, that's when I finally let go. My orgasm crashes into me as he collapses against my body, and I experience wave after wave of euphoria emptying into the condom.

He kisses me softly and looks into my eyes, and I swear I see the words that he wants to say but doesn't.

*I don't either. But goddamn, do I feel them.*

# Adrian

I can't get used to this. I mean I *could* definitely get used to this, but I'm afraid to. Waking up with Nash. Going to sleep in his arms. Spending time with his family, who are all absolutely incredible. Yeah, I shouldn't get used to this.

*It's all too damn good.*

And probably far more than I deserve, but I still want it desperately.

Samantha hasn't posted on social media at all, which is strange. Almost eerie. Although, she has called me several times. I haven't answered, but she sends texts, begging me to take her back, saying things will be different. I haven't listened to the voicemails, but I'm sure it's more of that. No part of me wants to go back to that life, and I never will.

My parents haven't called, which is also unnerving.

I'm certain Samantha hasn't told anyone what's happened, or I would have many, many messages from my father. But my mom knows we broke up. Surely my father will have something to say about that.

"Adrian, your dad's calling."

*Of fucking course. Speak of the devil himself.*

Three days. It took him three days after Samantha and I officially broke up to call and yell at me. Must have been a busy week.

"Ignore it and get in here with me," I yell over the sound of the shower raining down around me.

It's only a moment later that Nash, in all his naked glory, is climbing into the shower with me. "Damn." I shamelessly ogle him, and he laughs, shaking his head and grabbing body wash, lathering himself up.

He turns away from me, going under the shower head and giving me an excellent view of his glorious backside. I can't help but wonder as my eyes trail over the swell of his ass if he still bottoms sometimes. Or if he has since we were together so long ago.

*Maybe he didn't like it then. Maybe he's a pure top now. Or maybe that's only with me.*

He turns to face me again, wiping the water out of his eyes. "You're thinking hard again."

He pulls me to him and kisses my lips softly, and I blurt out, "Do you ever bottom?"

He laughs, and it surprises me how easily it comes from his mouth. And then I feel a sting of embarrassment, but he only kisses my forehead in response and grips my ass with his big hands. "I wasn't sure if you were a strict bottom now or not."

I shake my head. "I haven't been with anyone else, and I definitely like your cock in my ass." I feel said cock jerk between us in response and peck his lips. "But I wouldn't mind being inside you."

"Wouldn't mind, huh?" He raises an eyebrow.

My own cock is hard between us too. "Nuh-uh. Not at all."

He grins and pulls me into him again, kissing me hard and leaving me breathless. "I'd like that too." He nips on my bottom lip and then moves to kiss and suck on my neck. "I wouldn't mind you and only you inside of me. Nothing between us."

I moan, hearing what he's not saying. "You mean . . ."

"Bare." We grind against each other.

"Jesus. Why the fuck don't we have lube in here?" He chuckles, but it turns into a moan when he wraps his large hand around us both.

It doesn't take long before we're both spilling over his hand, especially with the thought of being inside him in my head. After we cleanup and dry off, we dress in his room, and I look at my phone.

Three missed calls. A voicemail. And a text telling me to call my father.

"You going to call him back?" Nash asks as he drags a shirt on over his head.

"Nah, I know where he is." I pull my shoes on as I sit on the edge of his bed. "I think I'm going to go to D.C. to tell him. I need to book a flight."

"When?"

I look up at him, nerves kicking in, but I hope I'm hiding them. "Tonight. I don't want him showing up here." I stand and cup his face in my hands. "I know you said you wanted to be there—"

"I do."

I smile and press a quick kiss to his lips. "You really don't have to. I can handle this."

Even though the thought of facing my father has me literally shaking. I mean what I said that I'm going to do it, and I don't want Nash to have any more ugliness in his life. My father can be vicious.

His hands move to my shoulders, and mine are still on his face. We're locked in our stance. "If you're going, I'm going with you. You shouldn't be alone to face that."

I smile and kick myself again for ever leaving this man. "Okay. I'll book a flight for both of us as soon as possible." I pull away and look out the window at the landscape outside, covered in snow. "This place is so beautiful. I don't want him showing up here and ruining it."

Nash's arms wrap around me from behind, and a smile forms on my lips, despite my apprehension about seeing my father. "He can't ruin this for us. We're together. That's all that matters, and if you aren't ready . . ."

I spin in his arms to look back at him. "I'm ready. I'm more than ready."

He smiles, and I think he believes me. "Okay." He kisses me softly, and I let myself get lost in him.

*This is where I want to be. This is who I want to be.*

*And I won't let anyone or anything ruin it ever again.*

ADRIAN IS NERVOUS. Hell, I'm nervous for him. I haven't been around his father much, but I know, from the few interactions I've had, I don't like him. "You sure you want to do this now?"

I look deep into Adrian's hazel eyes as we stand outside his father's office. He nods his head slowly, but I look down to see his hands are visibly trembling. I take his right hand in mine and bring it to my mouth, kissing his palm.

"You don't have to do this."

"I want to." The determination shines fiercely in his eyes as he brings his hand to my cheek and keeps it there. "I want this. And I can do this."

"Yes. You can. I just . . ." I take a deep breath, trying hard not to think about all those years ago when I thought he was going to run away with me. "I don't want you to feel like you have to."

He smiles. "I do have to." I'm sure I look confused, and he only smiles bigger. "For me. And for you. I want this life."

I nod, feeling comforted by his earnest tone. "Okay."

He kisses me chastely before pulling away, walking to the door, and opening it without even knocking.

I guess we're doing this.

His father sits behind his large oak desk, clearly startled at first but then quickly becoming angry. "Adrian. What are you doing here?"

"You called."

His eyes narrow in Adrian's direction, cold and furious. "I did. You didn't call back. Samantha is heartbroken. You ended things with her without explanation."

Adrian's back stiffens, and he stands taller even though I can see his nerves showing. "I gave her an explanation."

"Is that so?" He glances my way briefly, but then his eyes dart back to Adrian. "And what was that? Because the version I heard was that you kicked her out of someone else's resort and told her it was over. The poor girl is distraught."

I'm sure she is. Her perfect fantasy world—or her family's fantasy —was shattered.

"Yes." Adrian's voice doesn't waiver, and I'm oddly proud. "I'm gay."

Holy. Shit. He just went for it.

I think we're both holding our breath, just staring at his father and waiting for what I'm sure will be an abhorrent reaction. He's silent for far too long.

"Gay?"

Adrian nods, his shoulders back and spine straight. "Yes. I'm gay, and I never loved Samantha. She's not what I want. This life is not what I want."

His father stares at him, sitting perfectly still, and then he lets out a cruel laugh. "You are not gay. You're a drama queen, but you're not gay."

My fists clench at my sides, and I remind myself to take a deep breath. Adrian is a grown man, and this is his battle. I'm only here for support.

"I'm not going to argue with you." Adrian shakes his head. "I'm gay. And Samantha and I are not together."

"You will be if you know what's good for you, Adrian. You will call that girl and apologize. Right. Now."

I'm tense as hell, but I remain quiet.

"No." I feel relieved at Adrian's stern reply. Not that I doubted him. "And I quit."

His father stands now, placing his hands on the desk in front of him. "You can't quit. This is a family. You can't quit family."

"I can. And I do. I quit. Because this isn't a family. This is a dictatorship where I'm not allowed to be myself. And I'm not doing it anymore."

I want to cheer. Jump up and down, full-on cheer. I've never felt that urge in my life, but right now I want to.

"What will you do without us? Without me paying all your bills and without your prestigious last name, you're nothing, Adrian."

I step closer now, standing right at Adrian's side because I know this is exactly where all his doubt before came from. This. Man. Telling him for so long that he was nothing if he went against his father's plan for him, and I won't stand for it.

"I don't care about any of it. Take it all."

His father scoffs, his eyes flicking to me with rage, but he focuses back on Adrian. "You won't last. Where will you stay? Everything of yours is actually mine."

"He can stay with me." My voice is louder than I intend, but I'm pissed and barely keeping it together.

"You?" Now I have his father's full attention. "You're the staff at that place."

He says "place" as if it's a disease, but I ignore it. "My brother's cabins. Yes. And Adrian can stay with me."

"I can?" Adrian's eyes meet mine with a hopeful expression that nearly wrecks my heart.

"If you want that. Yes. I want you to move in with me."

He smiles, his chest puffing out a little as he turns to his dad. "I'll live with Nash."

"Nash." My name is said with malice as his father redirects his sight on me. "And what exactly do you want, Nash?" He turns to Adrian. "Men like this always want something. You'll learn that really quick."

I wince internally, thinking about the past. Thinking about when Lawson first met Raelynn. She was a rich girl from the other side of the tracks, and I thought she just wanted a fling with him—the bad boy from the wrong side.

And for a while, I thought that's all I was to Adrian.

But I was wrong. Not all rich people are like that, I've learned. Rae is the purest human I've ever met, despite her upbringing.

Before I can tell his dad where to shove his pompous assumptions, Adrian speaks up, grabbing my hand in his. "He wants me. And I would sell my goddamn soul just to be with him if I had to. But I don't have to." His voice cracks slightly as he squeezes my hand tighter. "But I don't have to with him. All I have to do is be myself. And that's what I'm going to do from now on."

My heart fucking soars. Tries to flat-out escape from my chest because yes, that's all I've ever wanted. Adrian turns to me, cups my face in his hands, and kisses me fervently. Telling me everything I need to know in one hot kiss.

"I love you."

I can barely catch my breath when his words hit my ears and I process it. "I love you too."

"Jesus Christ."

We both turn back to Adrian's dad as Adrian grabs my hand again and gives him a great big smile. "I quit. I never want to see you again." He releases my hand for a second and walks up to his father's desk. "And if you try to fuck with Nash or anyone in his family, I promise you the same thing I promised Samantha—I will take you down. And believe me, being around here—being a fly on the wall for years—I know plenty about you. Don't push me to make it ugly because I will —in a heartbeat."

His father swallows hard and looks pale as Adrian stares him down. "You wouldn't betray your family."

"You aren't my family." He looks back at me over his shoulder. "*He's* my family." He turns his focus back to his father. "Don't fuck with my family."

His father is clearly shocked, and I can't blame him because hell, I'm a little shocked myself. And turned-on. I mean, can't-wait-to-drag-him-back-to-the-hotel turned the hell on.

"I don't ever want to see you again either. As far as I'm concerned, I have no son."

Adrian doesn't falter. He only stands taller. "Sounds good to me because you were never a father."

*He takes my hand and pulls me with him, turning his back on the man who was supposed to be his dad and leaving him behind for good.*

# Adrian

MY BODY IS BUZZING with so much energy I feel like I might lift off the ground or collapse all at the same time. I've never felt so free in my life. There's no love lost with my father. Walking out of his office, and essentially his life, is the best thing I've ever done.

His words didn't sting. They really didn't. They were empty, hateful words that meant nothing to me. Because I realized he means nothing. And I've never been anything more to him than a pawn in the games he plays.

My hand is in Nash's as we ride in the elevator up to our hotel room with a family of four, complete with two rowdy kids bouncing up and down the whole time. The parents look exhausted but happy as they smile and apologize for their kids. And my mind briefly wonders if that's what Nash wants. If he wants to build a family.

Because with him, I'd be all for it. Even if I'd be terrified to mess it up. But somehow, I know, with Nash there guiding me along, I'd be an okay dad. He'd be the best.

When we finally reach our room, our lips fuse together before the door clicks closed. We're all tongues and hands, ripping each other's clothes off as we make it to the bed, my body landing under his.

"Do you want kids?"

Nash makes sort of a shocked noise as he lifts up, his weight resting on his hands, looking down at me. "That's what you're thinking about when we're both naked?"

I can't help the laugh that escapes me. "Apparently, I just blurt out anything these days."

He smiles now too, his lips moving back to mine and then sliding down my neck. His beard scrapes against my skin and makes me wonder why the fuck I was talking at all as I thrust against him. "Yes. I do. I think." His lips move to my ear as he uses his teeth to nip at my lobe. "I didn't ever think about it or really anything about the future, but now . . ." I close my eyes as his warm breath tickles my ear. His mouth slides over my jaw and then caresses my neck. "Now, I want everything. Adventures. Quiet nights in our cabin. Kids. Pets. All of it."

"Pets, huh?"

I feel him chuckle as his lips ghost over my chest. "That's the dealbreaker? Pets? Not children? You know kids are much louder, messier, everything-er."

"That's not a word." I open my eyes and grip the sides of his head, pulling him back up to me.

"It totally is."

"No dealbreakers for me. I'm all in, Nash. I want it all too."

He nods, his nose brushing mine before his mouth finds my lips again. We kiss and writhe against each other, our cocks slick with precum as we grind together. "I want you inside me. I can't stop thinking about it since you mentioned it in the shower."

I haven't either. "Okay." Lame, I know, but it's the only word I can get out with his large body on top of mine. I'm aching to be inside him.

"Bare." My breath hitches before I nod dumbly, unable to form any words. He mentioned that before, and I was tested after finding out Samantha was fucking other people. I trust him. And the fact that he trusts me is everything.

"Okay."

He grins, apparently amused at how dumbstruck the prospect of fucking him has made me. He moves off the bed, going to his back and grabbing a bottle of lube while I take the moment to admire the man before me.

He's all hard muscle and pure beauty as he saunters over to me and crawls back onto the bed. "I can't wait to feel you inside me again."

"How long has it been?"

"When was the last time we were together?"

"No." I sit up on my elbows. "I mean . . ." Suddenly, I feel way too vulnerable, but I force myself to ask. "Since you . . . ?"

He shakes his head at me, smiling big and beautiful. "Same answer. I haven't let anyone else inside me. I haven't been with another man."

That shocks me. I don't know why. I'm equally thrilled and saddened by that. Because I took that from him. I took intimacy and pleasure away from him for so long. "You haven't been with anyone else?"

He moves over my body, although my erection has flagged with the seriousness of the conversation. But it starts to perk back up at the feeling of his body blanketing mine. "I've been with women, but not another man."

"Why were you with women?" I'm not really sure what I'm feeling. Confusion? Jealousy? "Why would you have to hide?"

His hand moves through my hair as one hand holds him up, keeping some of his weight off me. "I wasn't hiding. I . . ." His eyes search mine, and I see he's deep in thought. "I enjoyed being with women. At least for a few hours. I hate labels. I don't really know what I am, but I guess I'm bisexual if I had to call it something."

"Oh." Dumb. That's a dumb response.

"Is that okay?" There's a smirk on his lips, but I detect vulnerability there too.

"Yes. Of course." I lean forward and kiss him softly before pulling back. "I mean, it doesn't matter anymore, right? It's just you and me?"

He looks hurt by my question, and I feel instantly guilty. He isn't Samantha. This isn't a fake, power-hungry business relationship. This is us. Nash and me. "Yes. Right?"

He sits back on his knees, and I hate that I'm fucking this up. "Nash, I . . ."

"You think I would cheat on you? Why? Because I like both men and women, and you think I need both? Or is it because of Samantha and the toxic shit she did?"

"Definitely option two." I sit up, moving to him and wrapping my arms around his neck. "But not at all either. I know you won't cheat on me. I don't know why I even let that come out of my mouth. I know you, Nash."

He nods, our foreheads touching as we both take a moment, sitting there on the bed, breathing in and out slowly. "I was never really with anyone else. When the loneliness got to be too much, I'd go to a bar and hookup. But that was it. I didn't lay there and talk afterward. I didn't talk about the future or kids or pets. I didn't talk at all. You were always in the back of my mind, even when I wanted to hate you."

I pull my head back and cup his face in my hand. "I'm sorry. I'm so sorry that I left you lonely and angry."

His hand covers mine and he laughs. "This is the least sexy foreplay we've ever had."

I bark out a laugh and shake my head. "Yeah. It's pretty bad."

He moves closer to me, his lips so close to mine that I lose track of everything we were talking about before. "It's also kind of the best because it's real. Because *you're* real. This is everything I could ever want, and I love you."

"I love you. God, Nash. I love you so damn much. I can't believe we're here. It feels like I'm going to wake up at any second."

"When you wake up, I'll be there. From now on, you're stuck with me."

"That's the least scary threat I've ever heard."

He chuckles but then nips at my bottom lip, and my body is back to being 100 percent back on board. "No more talking," he growls against my mouth, and yup, my dick is ready for him, hard and begging for me to shut the hell up.

I push him back against the bed and cover his body with mine now. "You're mine."

I nip over his neck and down his chest, sucking his nipple into my mouth and eliciting the sexiest groan from his throat I've ever heard. "Yes. Yours."

I kiss over his rigid abs that flex with every swipe of my tongue and brush of my lips. "Your body is mine."

"Yes." I move down, ignoring his cock that's flushed red and angry, weeping at the tip and begging for my mouth. "Please."

I ignore his pleas and move to his inner thigh, nipping at the flesh there and making him whimper with need. "Mine."

"Yes." I move to his balls, licking and sucking, driving him wild and torturing myself in the process. "Adrian." I smile against his sac, and he must feel it. "You're fucking evil."

I don't say a word, sucking his heavy balls into my mouth and making him writhe as saliva drips from my mouth and sliding down lower. When I release his balls, I follow the trail toward his hole, licking and circling it with my tongue as he thrusts up and spreads his legs, lost in pleasure.

"Please. Fuck. I need you."

To make a guy like Nash lose his mind is the ultimate high, and I'm so damn close already, I have no idea how I'm going to last when I'm inside him. I reach blindly for the lube as I use my tongue and finger to loosen him for me. After applying a generous amount of lube on my fingers, I slowly stretch him with one and then quickly insert a second finger.

"Now. I need you now."

I insert a third finger. "I don't want to hurt you." He hisses at the burn but still moves his hips, fucking himself on my fingers as I try like hell to gain my composure and not come on the sheets before I even get inside him.

"I like needy Nash."

"Umpfh." Yeah, that's not a word.

I remove my fingers and climb up his body to kiss his lips instead of pointing that out. "Are you sure about this? That you want my dick inside you?"

He knows I'm teasing him now and humps upward, dragging his cock against mine, making us both moan loudly. And again, I'm afraid I'm going to blow my load. "Get inside me now."

I grab the lube, unable to tease him more or come up with any retort. I slather the slickness over my aching cock and then press against his hole, not going inside. "I'm not going to last long inside you."

"I don't care." He wraps his hands around my ass and pulls me forward, pushing the tip of my dick inside his tight heat.

"Holy shit."

"Keep going." He's wanting and desperate.

I push inside, slowly inching my way in as his body tries to keep me out at first, but then he finally gives in, allowing me to slide inside and bottom out. "Jesus."

His big hands grip my ass now, holding me there, and I don't dare move as I'm surrounded by him and fully seated inside him. I can barely breathe as his ass squeezes me and holds me in the tight vice of his body.

"Nash."

"Kiss me." I do. I lean forward and ravage his warm mouth. "Now. Move." I happily follow his orders as he tops from the bottom. I pull back until I'm almost completely out of him and then thrust inside, his hands guiding me. "Yes."

We gasp and moan as we move together, and I try my best to keep it together. But it's not long before I feel the familiar tingle going up my spine, and I swear I nearly black out from the impending pleasure trying to break through.

My hand goes between us, still slick from prepping him, and I wrap it around his big cock, stroking furiously and hoping I can get him there before me. "You feel so good, Nash. So fucking good. How did we go so long without this? Without each other?"

"I don't know." He squeezes around my cock, and I know he's getting close. His voice is hoarse as he says, "But we're never doing it again."

"No. Never. You're mine. And I'm yours." I lean back, thrusting into him at the perfect angle I know will hit his prostate as I jerk his cock. I'm about to give in and come when I hear his strangled moan, his ass squeezing me even tighter as the warmth of his cum slides over my hand. "Thank fuck."

I let go as he thrusts into my hand, and I pound into his ass, my cock jerking with my own release, spilling cum deep inside of him.

"Damn." I collapse on top of him and laugh at his exasperation.

"Yeah."

He brushes a kiss against my temple. "This is everything I could have ever wanted."

"I can't believe we're here." And I can't.

"I'll be here when you wake up for the rest of our lives if you'll let me, Adrian." He knows how to reassure me.

"I'll be here too. I'm never making a stupid mistake when it comes to you ever again."

We share a brief kiss before we give in to total blissed-out exhaustion.

*How I came back from making the stupidest decision I've ever made, I'm still not sure. But I'm grateful for the second chance.*

*And I won't waste it.*

# Nash

I HOLD Adrian's hand as we walk into the dining hall that's filled with people for the Thanksgiving buffet Rae and Law planned. It smells incredible, and I'm grateful we weren't missed when we took a couple of extra days in D.C. to ourselves.

I haven't traveled much in my life. Pretty much just stayed in Texas until Lawson called and asked me to come to Missouri, but Adrian has a lot of experience in that area. It was strange, me wanting to go out and explore and him wanting to stay in the little cocoon we'd built in our hotel room.

We compromised, splitting time between the hotel and going out into the city, but it wasn't a fair split. Staying in with him was far too tempting, and I happily took less time out and about. But it's really good to be home.

And this is our home.

Hayden sees us first and heads over to us with a big grin on his face. I've caught him up on the events of our trip over text messages, and it's clear he couldn't be happier for me. He's a great friend, that much I'm sure of. "You guys finally made your way out of your sex comas to be here with us on a holiday?" He covers his heart mockingly. "I'm touched."

I roll my eyes but pull him into a hug. "Adrian said we had to come back. I would have run far away."

"Lies." He hugs me and then pushes me away. Lawson and Rae

move to us, and we catch up as the guests help themselves to a traditional Thanksgiving feast. Adrian and I sit down with them and eat as we go over plans for Christmas. Rae wants to have a Christmas Eve party, and I'm in a good enough mood to totally agree with her.

I feel like I have something to celebrate, and I'm all for it.

"Not to bring us all down or make it weird . . ." Rae looks nervous when she speaks up. I was in mid-bite of my mashed potatoes but place my fork down, my hackles rising.

"What's wrong?"

"Nothing," she says hesitantly.

My brow crinkles, and I feel Adrian tense next to me.

"Nothing?"

She shakes her head, looking anxious. "That's the thing. I haven't seen a post on Samantha's account since before she left."

Adrian is still tense, and I hear him suck in a big breath and let it out. "She's called and texted me, wanting to get back together. But I know it's weird that she hasn't posted. She's always posted multiple times daily since I met her, even when she had the flu."

Rae is gnawing on her bottom lip as she listens. "Yeah. So that's either really bad . . . or good, I guess? Right? I mean, she's either plotting something horrible or she's run off to lick her wounds, never to be heard from again."

Hayden snorts and then wraps his arm around Raelynn. "Oh, sweet Rae. That girl will be back. She craves attention."

I know he's right. It's been easy to live in our happy little bubble after she left, but I know something will happen with her eventually. That story isn't over yet.

"I don't think she'll do anything. I tried my best to make sure nothing happens, Raelynn." Adrian sounds sad and guilty, and I get it, but it's not his fault. None of us wanted to let him live in that prison any longer.

Thankfully, Rae expresses my thoughts before I have to. She reaches out, covering Adrian's hand with her own. "I don't care what happens. I'm glad you did what you did. And if you guys wouldn't have told me what a garbage human she was, I would have kicked both your asses when I found out. Because the truth always comes out."

Adrian eyes her with amusement and admiration, and I smile because that's how I feel around Rae. "I don't want you guys hurt because of my mistakes."

She shrugs and pulls her hand back to her lap. "It's the wondering that's driving me crazy. I'm just ready to deal with whatever she's going to do head-on."

"You're brave," Adrian observes astutely.

Lawson grins as he kisses her temple from his seat next to her. "You have no idea."

I turn to look at Adrian, and his eyes meet mine. "It's going to be okay. Whatever happens, we can handle it."

Adrian nods, and Hayden pipes up, changing the subject. "So, how was the sex? Good, right? It's got to be totally explosive with the two of you. I mean, with all the sexual tension and built-up repression, it had to be so damn good. Was it good?"

I laugh because he's way too excited, and I grab a roll, tossing it at him. "Wouldn't you like to know?"

He catches the roll and takes a bite out of it, chewing. "Hell, yeah. Details. I need them. All of them. Every single hot, sweaty second."

Rae shakes her head and hugs him to her. "Never change."

"Couldn't if I tried, Rae."

*We all laugh at that. But truthfully, there's no one at this table I want to change a damn thing about.*

# *Adrian*

It's been two weeks since Thanksgiving, and everything has been so damn amazing. I mean, it's almost too good. I haven't heard from Samantha or my parents. There have been no news stories or posts about me or the cabins.

It's been peaceful and hectic at the same time because I've been helping as much as I can around here, and they're still packed to capacity.

It's evening now. Nash, Hayden, and I built an awesome room that's essentially a spacious den, complete with a fireplace and several comfortable seating areas where guests can gather and hang out in the evenings. There's an enormous television as well as a hot cocoa bar. A huge picture window is perfectly placed so you can stare out at the snow as it falls and covers the trees.

If you'd have asked me months ago what my version of Heaven was, I don't think I'd have ever come up with this scenario. But as I sit here on one of the plush couches, Nash's arm around me, and mug of hot cocoa in my hand, I know this is it. Rae and Lawson are cuddled up too while Hayden and Tammy play a game of foosball.

"You okay?" Nash's deep voice is a husky whisper in my ear, reminding me of the sinfully delicious things he did to me in the shower earlier this morning. I'm lost in the memory of him kneeling in front of me on the tile floor as water poured over his back when his voice turns to more concern. "Adrian?"

Right. Boyfriend. Talking. I turn to look at him. "I'm more than okay. I've never been better, Nash."

He grins and gives me a quick peck on the lips. "Stop it! You're making the single people all weepy," Hayden yells, and Nash feigns pity.

"You could be coupled-up too if you really wanted it. Don't pretend that's not true."

Hayden cackles at that before scoring a goal against Tammy in a totally cheap shot that has her squealing in fake anger. We all laugh, and I settle back into Nash's side. "It almost feels too good though," I say quietly, not wanting to pull anyone else into the doubt I'm feeling. But Nash is mine, and he has to deal with that now.

He does it well. His strong arm hugs me more tightly to him. "Nothing is too good."

My eyes look over at Rae and Lawson, who are lost in their own conversation, and then back to Nash. "I've never been this happy, but I can't shake the feeling that something is going to happen to make it all crash down around me. To ruin us."

"Nothing . . ." He grabs my chin with his other hand and forces me to look at him in his totally domineering Nash way that makes me feel safer than I've ever felt. "Nothing will ever ruin us. You have to get that out of your head. It doesn't matter what happens, we'll handle it."

I nod and lean forward, resting on his chest as he releases his grip on me. "I love you."

I feel him smiling. "I love you too."

We're lost in the moment, but when I hear the door pull open and a click of heels so distinctly familiar, my entire body goes rigid. Nash must see her too because his body goes from calm and relaxed to being on full-alert.

When I look up, sure enough, Samantha stands before us in a puffy pink coat and black leggings with snow boots. Still as fashionable as ever. She takes in the sight of Nash and me cuddled together in front of the fire, her eyes trailing over every detail. But strangely, she doesn't look furious.

I'm still full of nerves, however, at what her presence could mean.

*I really hate when I'm right.*

"What are you doing here?" I ask as I sit up straight and look up to where she's standing.

"I haven't posted since I left here."

That's a fact we're all aware of. "Yeah. I know. Why?" I'm cautious in my question, waiting for the other shoe to drop.

She looks around nervously. Hayden and Tammy stopped their game and have moved to stand behind the couch Nash and I are sitting on. Lawson and Rae have ended their conversation and are definitely paying attention. "I haven't posted since I left until . . ." She doesn't look full of chaos, but instead, she looks more frightened and nervous. "Until a few moments ago."

Shit.

"What did you do?" I glare at her.

She looks stunned for a moment but then shakes her head slowly, almost in a daze. "N-nothing. I mean, nothing bad." Nash's hand goes to my thigh and squeezes it slightly to show he's here, and her eyes track the movement. When her eyes meet mine again, I see unshed tears, but I don't feel sorry for her. "We broke up."

"I'm well aware of that. I was there." I stand up to face her head-on. "What did you do?"

She looks slightly confused and then reaches in her pocket, grabbing her phone and showing me the screen after she unlocks it. "I mean officially. We broke up." I look at the picture that's just of her, looking not too happy but not terribly upset either. "*Amicably.* I said that we wanted different things and left it vague. That our lives were going in different directions, and I want all the best for you."

She takes the phone back and places it in her pocket, before looking over at Rae. "I'm going to post a final review of the cabins tomorrow. I was hoping I could take one more picture here. I promise it will be honest."

Rae looks over at me, and I give her a look that I hope portrays it's completely up to her, and then she looks back at Samantha. "I'll have to look at that post you just made first."

Samantha wastes no time bringing her phone to Rae to let her read every word, and Nash stands at my side, pulling me closer. I happily lean into him. Rae hands Samantha's phone back to her. "You aren't going to suddenly change it?"

"No." Samantha looks more sincere than I've ever seen her, but we're all suspicious, I can feel it. Her tear-filled eyes look back to me. "I'm sorry. I know I acted badly. You know how we were raised, Adrian. I—"

"No," I quickly interrupt because this is something I know, without a doubt, is wrong with the world. "You can't blame it on how you were raised. It's a choice to be decent, and it's a choice to be awful. You're an adult, and you get to choose. Every day."

"I know." She lets out a quiet sob. "I'm trying to fix it. I know. I was wrong."

I want to believe her, but it's not easy. She takes in a deep breath and releases it. "I promise I'm going to make a beautiful post about this place tomorrow because it's special. It won't be a lie. It will only be the truth." She looks over at Raelynn and Lawson. "You two have built something very beautiful."

"I agree," I add. Samantha looks at me, wiping away a tear that's fallen, one I believe might be genuine.

"I needed to come back and tell you in person."

"Okay."

We take an awkward group picture in front of the fireplace with snow in the background, and she leaves. Just like that. With the promise she'll post it tomorrow along with a good review.

"Hmm, look at that." Nash kisses the side of my head. "We're still standing."

*And I know we always will be as long as we're next to each other.*

MY AXE SLICES through the wood effortlessly as Hayden works to add the split pieces to the pile and Adrian stacks more on my other side to be split next.

"It's super cute when couples start to look like each other."

Adrian stops stacking wood and looks down at his heavy winter coat and jeans. "We don't look alike."

Hayden smirks and gestures toward the brown work boots on Adrian's feet that are nearly identical to my black boots and then nods in the direction of his beautifully handsome face--which is now sporting a short beard. It's far shorter than mine and trimmed neatly. "Sure."

I can't help the laugh as I split another piece of wood and then look over at Adrian. "I think you look hot."

"That's because you look aliiiike." Hayden sings, and Adrian must agree on some level based on the next words out of his mouth.

"Your ego is as big as your dick," Adrian quips, and Hayden perks up.

"Please tell me more."

Adrian flips him off but is laughing as he does. "Stay off my boyfriend, Hayden."

"Fine. You keep your grumpy bear." Hayden sighs dramatically. "I'll just have to find one of my own."

"I'm sure you can around here. When was the last time you had a date?" Adrian asks as I keep working. There's a bonfire tonight, and it's cold as hell out here. We'll need plenty of firewood.

I don't miss the longing in Hayden's voice as he answers though. "Too long. I've been busy." He tries to play it off, but I think there's more to it. Since I've met him, he's joked and flirted a lot, but I haven't ever seen or heard about him being in a relationship.

"Maybe you should make some time for that," Adrian says what I'm thinking because a guy as great as Hayden deserves to have someone.

Hayden shrugs. "Eh. Then I'd be too busy to hang out with you two, and then what would you do?"

I split another piece of wood and then bury the ax in the stump to turn to Hayden. "I'm sure we'd find something."

"I don't know." Hayden picks up the wood from the ground and stacks it neatly. "I think you'd miss me."

"Just don't find anyone who makes you move from here, and we'll be good."

His nose, red from the cold, crinkles. "A local, huh?"

I nod, and Adrian grins at me. "Yes. A local would be great."

Rae and Law join us outside, carrying food and supplies for the bonfire. But they must have heard our conversation because Lawson shoves Hayden's shoulder. "You better never leave us. But I agree, you need to get out there. Find your keeper."

"Aw, it's funny you think someone could keep me," Hayden shoots back with a wink.

"It's not so bad being kept." Adrian leans his head against my shoulder.

"I agree." I smile, and Hayden makes a fake gagging noise.

"You all are gross now. I think I'll pass on the couple thing." We carry wood over to the spot we're having the bonfire, and Hayden places the last piece on top. "Although I wouldn't mind finding a dick to play with. Or two."

"You're a mess," I say with affection because I know it's a defense mechanism. For whatever reason, Hayden doesn't feel worthy of love.

Adrian goes inside with Rae and Law to get more food for the fire, leaving Hayden and me alone.

"You'll find someone."

"Or you and Adrian will let me be your third." He takes a seat as I start the fire, and I know he's kidding. His heart is barely in it and overridden by sadness.

"You don't need to be our third. You're going to find someone and be their entire world. Their fucking everything. You'll see."

He waves me off, but I see the longing in his eyes. But then, he's back to bouncy happy Hayden when the guests arrive and Tammy, Law, Rae, and Adrian come back outside. We eat and have smores and hot cocoa, all cuddled up around the fire. The guests seem to be having a good time. The bonfire was one of the things that was very popular during Samantha's stay here, so we'll be sure to keep it. I'm glad because it's probably my favorite thing.

She kept her word and posted a positive post the day after she showed up here. She said she was so disappointed she had to leave early, but she encouraged everyone to check out the cabins. It doesn't make up for anything she's done, in my opinion, but if she actually does work on herself, I guess that's a good thing. And there's no denying her post has only helped increase the popularity of this place. It's fully booked nearly entirely next year.

And I think about how damn lucky I got when Samantha or Samantha's father or whoever the fuck chose this place as their destination. Because I have Adrian.

He leans against me, that hungry look in his eyes as his mouth moves to my ear. "I'm having fun, but I can't stop thinking about all the things we could be doing in our cabin."

I grab his hand and stand up, looking at Lawson. "You're good, right? I think we're going to turn in."

Hayden snorts. "You two are so obvious."

Lawson laughs. "Go. Have fun."

I don't wait for more teasing from my family. Instead, I lead Adrian back to the cabin where we waste no time stripping down and finding the bed. I want to take my time, but I also can't wait to be inside him.

He's on the same page because before I know it, he has the lube and is prepping himself before replacing his fingers with my slick cock. "Jesus." I push inside him. "I'll never tire of this."

"You better not." He turns around, cocking his neck just enough to capture my lips with his in a punishing kiss as I thrust into him, holding onto his hips. He's added some muscle already from the hard work here at the cabin, but his body is still lithe and graceful as we move together.

One of his hands reaches for his cock as he jerks himself in time with each thrust of my throbbing shaft into his tight ass. "Fuck, Nash," he pants, and I know he's close.

"Come for me, Adrian. I want to feel this ass squeeze the life out of my cock when you do."

He makes an unintelligible grunt as his arm moves faster, and then he clenches around me so tight, I see stars and my own release hits me hard, pumping my cum inside him.

We're a sticky, sweaty mess when I collapse next to him, but neither of us move to clean up. We just lay there, my arm covering my eyes as we try to get our breathing under control.

"So good." He says it in a way like he almost can't believe it, and I know that feeling all too well.

I turn to my side and pull his naked body into mine. "It's only going to get better."

*How? I have no idea because it feels pretty damn perfect. But I know my words are true. With him here by my side, life can only get better and better.*

# Adrian

THE CHRISTMAS EVE party has been a tremendous success so far. Everyone is dressed up, and there's a live band along with all the tables pushed out of the way to make room for dancing for whoever wants to. I haven't heard from my parents or from Samantha, and it's been peaceful as hell.

And for whatever reason, I've stopped fearing all the bad things that could happen in the future.

I smile at Nash as we serve hot cocoa and cider to our guests, and I know, without a doubt, he's right about us being happy, no matter what the rest of our lives hold. We have each other. That's all I need.

And our cabin.

Who knows? Maybe a couple of kids someday to run around with Rae and Law's little bundle of joy. Yeah. Raelynn is pregnant now. She told us the news this morning with a great big grin, and I've never seen Nash happier.

He's going to be the best uncle and, maybe someday, a dad. Hayden joins us with freshly baked cookies and places them on the table. But he surprises me when he ducks down behind my legs. "Hayden?"

"Shhh." I look down at him, waiting for an explanation, and he shakes his head. "Don't look down here. Look up!"

Nash chuckles. "Are you really hiding from the cops?"

I turn to see what the hell he's talking about when I spot Tristan heading our way. He's a local cop, and his sister owns a resort on the

193

lake where Rae and Law first started working when they moved here. I've seen them both around occasionally, but I have no idea why Hayden is hiding.

"What did you do?" I ask him quietly.

"Nothing. Stop looking down here." He tries to shoo me away.

"Hayden?" Tristan's booming voice comes from right across the table, and there's no doubt he can see Hayden cowering behind me. "You okay?"

Hayden bounces up, wiping off his pants. "Yes. Of course." I think his voice sounds squeakier than usual, and I turn to Nash, an eyebrow raised in question.

He just shrugs like he has no idea and turns toward the cop, who's in full uniform from head to toe. "What are you up to tonight, Tristan?"

Tristan just looks around the party, his eyes darting around at all the guests, more curious than suspicious. Then he focuses back on us. "I heard there was a party. Thought I'd check it out."

"You? Party?" Hayden says, and yeah, his voice is still strangely different.

Tristan offers a bright white smile in Hayden's direction now, clearly amused. And maybe flirty? I'm not sure. From what I've heard, he's straight, but we all know how deceiving making assumptions can be. And labels for that matter.

"You don't want me here?"

"I didn't say that." Hayden smiles nervously, and it's funny to me because I've never seen him flustered before.

"I was actually looking for you. I need a favor."

Hayden looks like he wants to say something but can't and finally clears his throat loudly before he manages an "Oh, yeah?"

"Yeah. My sister is forcing me to go on a date this weekend, and I haven't been on a damn date for a long time. I thought maybe you could help me find something to wear, considering you're always commenting on my clothes."

"What?" Hayden laughs nervously. "I am not. I just said there are other colors besides black, but black suits you."

I think Hayden is blushing now, and I can't stop staring at this trainwreck happening in front of me. "Well, it's kind of the uniform."

"I've seen you out of uniform." Hayden is, without question, blushing now as he quickly adds, "I mean, I've seen you in swim trunks. Not that I was looking. I mean, you came to a hot tub party, and you were wearing snug black swim trunks." I don't think he takes a breath and then adds, "No, Not snug. I wasn't looking."

Nash casually moves over and places a hand on Hayden's shoulder, hushing him.

Tristan only laughs. "Right. Well, you aren't wrong. Most of my outfits are jeans and black t-shirts when I'm not working, and my only swim trunks are black. So, could you maybe help me?"

"Ummm." Hayden falters for a bit and then says, "Yeah. Of course. So, who's the lucky person?"

Tristian sounds casual. "Tammy."

"Tammy?" Another squeak from Hayden. "My Tammy? She hasn't said anything."

Tristian grips the back of his neck, looking a little sheepish himself. "Yeah. Well, she's friends with Amanda, and I don't know. I haven't been on a date in so damn long, I'm sure it won't amount to anything."

"That's great. Tammy's great. I mean, really great." I see Nash squeeze Hayden's shoulder, and Hayden looks grateful.

"Right. Well, maybe you can come over Saturday afternoon? I'm supposed to pick her up that evening."

Hayden resembles a bobblehead at this point, his head nodding over and over. "Yeah, sounds great. That would be great."

"Okay." Tristan seems happily amused before he thanks Hayden again and then goes to mingle with the crowd.

"Oh my God." Hayden covers his face with both hands. "What the hell is wrong with me?"

Nash grins. "I'd say you have a little crush on the cop."

He drops his hands. "No. No. No. He's straight. I'm not falling for a straight guy who'll probably punch me for drooling over him."

Nash's gaze darkens now. "He better fucking not." His voice

softens a little when he says, "But you know Tristan isn't like that. He's a good man."

"You've barely been around him."

"I know he helped you when you got stuck in that ditch last year. And he was fun at the hot tub party."

"I say go for it." I have to add my two cents.

"No way." He raises his hands in a surrender. "That's not going to happen. I'm going to help him put some damn color in his wardrobe and then send him on a date with Tammy. They'll make perfect little babies and be happy, and I'll die miserable and alone."

He sits down in a nearby chair in a huff, and I shake my head at him, trying not to laugh. "That seems pretty dramatic."

"Hello? I'm dramatic."

I do laugh now, and so does Nash. "I still say you should try. You don't know he's straight. Maybe he likes both men and women."

Hayden rolls his eyes. "Please. He screams straight."

"You thought the same about me," Nash says as he wraps an arm around my waist.

Hayden seems to be thinking about it for a moment, but then he hops up from his chair shaking his head. "Nope. Nope. Nope. I'm not going there. You guys can't make me." He leaves before either of us can say another word, and it makes us both laugh.

"Your best friend is crazy."

Nash only chuckles fondly. "You're stuck with him now too."

"Package deal."

"Yup. And no refunds."

I kiss him softly. "I don't want one."

"Good."

The rest of the night is everything I could ever want with Nash, Rae, Law, Tammy, and Hayden.

*I've found my family.*

Waking up with Adrian in my arms never gets old. Him being naked *really* never gets old. I feel him smiling against my bare chest, so I know he's awake too. "Merry Christmas."

"Merry Christmas, Adrian."

His hand moves down and covers my morning wood. "Is this my present?"

"Definitely." I smile into a kiss, but before we can get to anything else, I hear the front door open, and Hayden bursts in.

"Better hide anything good! But I did bring coffee!"

"Hayden." I lie back flat on my pillow, pissed about the cockblock, but not really because it's Hayden. "That key is for emergencies."

He appears in the doorway, and I can hear Rae, Law, and Tammy in the next room. "Listen, we called. And called. You two lazy fuckers need to get out of bed. It's Christmas morning!"

Adrian chuckles. "Can we get dressed first?"

Hayden huffs. "Fine." He turns around and closes the door behind him, giving us privacy. Adrian throws the covers off, climbing out of bed. I can't help noticing his dick is still semi-hard, and I mentally yell at Hayden again.

"Your friends have the worst timing."

"They're your friends too," I say, reluctantly sliding out of bed and pulling on a pair of sweats.

Adrian looks down at the still-there bulge. He walks over to me and cups me through the fabric. "I had plans."

I lean forward and kiss him. I'm trying to get my erection to go down, not regain interest, so I keep it chaste. "We'll definitely turn those plans into a reality tonight when we get them all to go away."

He grins at me and then begrudgingly gets dressed before we go out to greet everyone. They have a full breakfast spread out on the table, and I see Hayden wasn't lying about the coffee.

I give Rae a side hug, and she gives me a great big smile, even though she turns a little green when Hayden scoops eggs onto her plate. "No, thank you."

"Right. Eggs. Bad." Hayden slides them off her plate and onto his before trying bacon. "Bacon. Good?"

Rae laughs but still looks a little sick. It seems my little nephew or niece is giving her a hard time. "I think just toast."

"This kid." Hayden shakes his head, but he's smiling. I know he's as excited as the rest of us about Raelynn and Lawson bringing a kid into the world. I can't think of two better parents. I know that kid is going to be loved and taken care of, no matter what.

I release Rae and sit next to Adrian, trying to tell my mind to slow down because all I can think about is my future with him. About making him my husband and maybe having those kids we talked about.

I want it all with him, and I know we're on the same page. Soon. Very soon. But for now, I'm content just having him back in my life. And this time, I'm not letting him get away. I smile at my brother, who's fawning over Rae, trying to find her something else to eat, and then Hayden and Tammy, who are chatting about her impending date with the cop.

Next year, there'll be a baby here at Christmas. And who knows? Maybe I'll also talk Adrian into getting a dog. I never thought I'd be here. I thought living a simple life, keeping to myself and being a loner, was the best kind of life for me.

I believed as long as Lawson was happy, I'd be happy too. And for a long time, I was content, pushing away all my old memories and ignoring the longing I felt deep in my gut.

*But now, I see I can truly have it all.*

*And I do. Because I have him.*

# NOTE FROM THE AUTHOR

I hope you all enjoyed Nash and Adrian as much as I enjoyed writing about them! Their story meant everything to me. I hate hate hate the ugliness of the world and people who pretend to be kind, good people, but as it turns out, they aren't so nice. I can't stand it, but I firmly believe there is still good out in the world.

I believe people can change, but it takes work to make that change. It takes honestly examining yourself and trying to see the world and everyone in it from all angles. It's important to take a long look at ourselves and do the work we need to do to accept everyone as they truly are. I want the world to be a better place. I want there to be a time when no one has to come out at all. That you just love who you love, and that's all that ever needs to be said.

I'm grateful to all of you for reading my book! I hope you loved the story because I definitely enjoyed writing it. I love these characters, and they are so hard to let go. If you love Hayden, no worries—he is getting his own story very soon!

Thank you so much to my cover designer, Sarah, for the gorgeous cover for this book. Thanks also to Elizabeth for making the inside pretty! Thank you to Dena for cleaning up my words. I don't want to think about life without any of you!

Thanks to Ari, Elle, and Emma for always being there for me. You guys know I love you and stuff. To my family, I love you all. To my babies: thank you for just being you and know I'll always be proud of you no matter what! Be you.

And to my readers, bookstagrammers, bloggers, and Novelties: I adore each and every one of you!

Live your life. Be strong, but remember, it's okay to feel how you feel. You are valid, and so are your feelings. Be you. And be proud to be you. Never let hate and ugliness win because you are beautiful.

Love you all!

-Nicole

# IMMORAL PROLOGUE

**Ryan**

"What are you doing over here by yourself, loser?"

*Grady fucking Bell.*

I smile at the sound of my best friend's voice coming from behind me while I sit on the dock, staring at the rippling water in the moonlight. I'm holding onto the neck of a whiskey bottle resting between my legs, but I haven't had much to drink tonight. It's graduation night. I should be happy. I *am* happy.

My dreams are about to come true. So are his.

But those dreams are sending us in completely different directions.

I feel his body crowd mine as he takes a seat on the end of the dock with me, his sneakers dangling just above the water like my own. "There's an epic party going on right back there." He extends his lanky arm behind us, that bigass grin with his bright, white teeth visible in the night.

"Aren't you tired of partying yet, Grady?"

He laughs at that, effortless and contagious. Grady is larger than life. He was even when we were in second grade, never caring what

203

anyone thought about him. He can hit a home run effortlessly. Get an A on a test without even studying. Sing any song in existence acapella while bringing the biggest badass out there to tears. Score the winning touchdown in the last few seconds of a game. Play a song on his guitar perfectly after only hearing it once.

Grady Bell is a goddamn legend in this town, and now he's leaving.

"We're just getting started, Bailey."

I roll my eyes at the use of my last name but still smile because it's something he's always done. *Bell and Bailey.* In a small town like ours, that meant we were always paired together. School. Sports. Newspaper achievements.

*Always.*

"Seems to me, *Bell*, that we *were* just getting started, but then you had to go and sign with a record label."

He gives me a sly grin and steals the whiskey bottle from between my thighs, even though I can smell the booze on him already. "You want me to tell them to fuck off?" I turn to look at him and that intoxicating grin on his face. "Because I fucking will."

I laugh and look out at the lake water again. We both had baseball scholarships to the same college. That was the plan. It's always been my plan, decided for me before I was even born by a father with the same dream for himself.

Unfortunately, my mom got pregnant in an "oops" situation during their senior year of high school, and my dad proposed, then immediately went to trade school to learn to be a welder. I think it was then he decided I would be the baseball player.

And I'm not half bad.

Grady, the talented motherfucker, is good at all he does and, of course, excelled at baseball along with everything else. So, we decided that was our ticket out of this town. The major leagues. We'd play for the big boys, party like crazy, buy our moms houses, and never come back to this small town.

But instead, he had to go and get signed with a record label who wants him to immediately go to LA and lay tracks for an album. I'm happy for him. Music has always been his favorite talent, but I'm a selfish asshole feeling lost and abandoned.

"No." I turn to look at Grady, his black hair just a little overgrown and blowing in the wind, and even though I can't see his dark green eyes, I know they're sparkling with mischief. "I want you to go and blow their fucking minds."

His grin widens. "You know I will. And you?"

I shrug and swallow hard, still facing him. "Me?"

"You're going to kill it in college sports, and then you're going to the MLB. You're going to the big leagues, and they won't even know what hit them."

*How can I do that without Grady?*

*What's a catcher without his pitcher?*

I don't recognize my own voice as I shift my body so I'm facing him directly, pulling my legs up on the dock and tucking them under me awkwardly. "What if I fail?"

He places the whiskey bottle next to him and then turns his body, mimicking my position. His large hands grip my face, not letting me look away. "Ryan, when have you ever failed in your life?"

*When hasn't he been there to back me up?* It's what I want to ask, but I don't. I just shake my head, taking his hands with me as I do. "I'm scared."

I hate making this admission. Men don't get scared. And if we do, we sure as hell don't admit it. In a small town like this in Kansas, men are still supposed to be "tough." We don't show weakness. "Me too."

I'm shocked when he readily admits this. Grady isn't afraid of anything. "You'll be fine."

"I'm going to California, Ry. This is all I've ever known." He doesn't release me, but he looks around the lake. No one is around us, but I hear the music coming from the shabby cabin our class rented for the weekend, and I can see the bonfire they started close to it. "You'll be great."

His eyes meet mine, and I feel that familiar feeling stirring low in my belly. One I've been trying to ignore for years. One I've tried to drink away. I've tried my best to get lost in the girls in our class and out on the baseball field. I've thrown myself into everything else, trying like hell to ignore the one thing I know deep down I want.

*Him.*

"So will you."

"Chances of going pro are slim," I say lamely, my eyes transfixed on his full lips. No wonder he has such a reputation for being a good kisser. With lips like those, how could he not be?

Of course, that's only with girls.

Every fucking girl in our school.

*Grady is, no doubt, straight. And I . . . I have no idea what I am.*

*Lost.*

That seems about right.

He cups the back of my neck with one of his hands and pulls me close, resting his forehead against mine in a gesture he's done a lot when I've doubted myself. "Not for you. You're Ryan fucking Bailey. You're going to go far. You were destined for this."

A shiver runs through me from the intensity of his eyes on mine. "You're always so sure."

"About you? Of course, I am."

I want to lean in even closer. I breathe him in and hope like hell it's not noticeable, but I can't resist. He smells like whiskey and the lake from swimming earlier. And him. Just fucking him.

"Grady?" My voice is full of gravel as he pulls back enough to look into my eyes. His breathing seems rapid, but maybe it's my imagination.

"Yeah?"

I swear his gaze drops to my lips, but I try to shake that thought away. I've wanted him for years, but there's no way he feels the same. "I don't know what I was going to say," I admit.

"You think too much, Bailey. You always have." His thumb on his free hand—the other is still cupping the back of my neck—runs over my bottom lip, and I think I stopped breathing.

When he leans closer to me, I'm almost certain I'm dreaming. Or maybe I fell into the lake and am drowning. *Hell, maybe I'm dead.*

But when his firm lips press against mine, I couldn't give a fuck if I'm actually dead because this is my heaven.

His hand around the back of my neck grips me tighter and pulls me closer as a growl escapes my throat, and I don't think . . . I just attack his mouth with mine. Taking everything I've wanted for so damn long.

My hands move to his thick, soft hair, threading my fingers through it and pulling him to me, not able to get close enough. His mouth opens for me as my tongue darts inside, tasting Grady. *Finally.*

*God, he tastes good.*

Our moans mingle as he shoves me onto my back on the dock, and I think this is it. This is when he'll wake up from his drunken daze and punch me right in the face.

But he doesn't.

Instead, his body covers mine, settling between my legs, and I know he can feel how hard I am. But what really fucking shocks me to my core, something I'll never forget for as long as I live, is the erection that's *not* mine. His hard dick is pressed against mine as our lips meet again, and we grind against each other. Groaning and moaning with need as we kiss and writhe on the old wooden dock. My body is larger than his—both in pure muscle mass and in height—but he has no problem taking control, grabbing both my hands and pinning them above my head as our clothed cocks rub against each other, and I'm about to lose my mind.

"Grady," I gasp, close to coming in my jeans.

He pulls back enough to look down into my eyes, not releasing his hold on me. "Yeah?"

"What are we doing?"

I could kick myself for stopping this, but this is Grady. He doesn't make out with guys. *I can't be a drunken mistake. Not to him.*

"Celebrating?" His right eyebrow kicks up along with a cocky grin spreading on his too handsome face.

I'm shocked he isn't flipping the fuck out. But again, this is Grady. He doesn't freak out. He's calm, cool, and collected. Always. It's why he's a fucking fantastic pitcher. Nothing rattles him. "Like this?" I rasp as I feel his body on top of mine while I pant and plead with him silently to come back to me.

The spell broken, he sits up, letting go of my wrists and kneeling between my legs. "Maybe not the best idea."

It's like a knife plunging into my heart, but deep down I know he's right. There are so many things I want to say to him. I want to pull him back to me, kiss the fuck out of him, and tell him I'm an idiot for saying anything. To get lost with me.

But I don't. Instead, I take his hand when he stands and then pulls me up, ruffling my hair in the casual, easy way that's just Grady.

He isn't freaking out that he kissed a guy. His thoughts aren't swirling around in his head that's moving far away while I'm staying in the same state where we grew up. He doesn't worry about any of that.

"Come on, fucker. This is our last night before the real world comes calling and we make it our bitch."

I follow, but it's on shaky, uncertain legs.

*Because now, I've had a fucking taste. And I have no idea how I'm going to come back from that.*

**Like what you read? Grab Immoral on Amazon! Free with Kindle Unlimited!**
Immoral - Kindle edition by Dykes, Nicole. Literature & Fiction Kindle eBooks @ Amazon.com.

# SNEAK PEEK

Rather have a single father/kindergarten teacher romance? Go to the next page for a peek at Totally Schooled!

# TOTALLY SCHOOLED

## Chapter 1

### Rafe

"Daddy! Are we going to school now?" I grin at my daughter, who just bounced into our living room, her blond hair a total wreck from her nap. "Pleeeeasse."

I laugh at her, swiping her hair behind her ear and pulling her onto my lap. "In a minute."

"Yes!" She's so damn excited to go to kindergarten this year. It will be her first time in school, and although I'm excited for her, I'm also scared as hell. She's never been in the care of anyone she wasn't related to before.

"It's just to meet your teacher this evening though. You know that, right?"

Her little bottom lip pokes out like it does when she's thinking hard about something. "Yeah. That's okay. My teacher is going to be awesome."

I laugh, I can't help it. I'm definitely not a laugher, but when it comes to Hailey, I laugh. I joke. I play. Hell—I'm a princess when she tells me I'm a princess and we're going to have a tea party with her dolls. I'll do anything for the kid. "Yeah. I'm sure she'll be really nice, sweetie."

Or at least, Ms. Burke had better be nice or my ass will be out of that school so fast. I try to shake away my nerves. I know this is part of the whole parenting thing, but I've come to terms with this being the hardest part of parenting for me a long time ago.

Trusting someone else with Hailey.

Other than my Aunt Jo, I don't let anyone watch her.

*Guess that's all changing now.*

I move Hailey to the floor in front of me so I can try to wrangle her hair into a ponytail. It's a mess of curls—just like her mother had. My heart clenches in my chest when I think about Heather, but I try my best to put a smile on my face by the time Hailey jumps up, turns around, and grabs my hand. "Okay, Daddy. Let's go."

"Yeah? You sure you want to go to school?"

She puts one hand on her hip, cocking it an angle and giving me the stink eye. "Yes. Let's goooooo."

I chuckle, and we walk outside of our small apartment. I lock the door before Hailey drags me down two flights of stairs to my car. I unlock the car, buckle her into her car seat, and drive to the school. We've driven past it several times in the last two days since we moved to Shawnee, a Kansas City suburb.

The school is close to our apartment, so it doesn't take long to get there. As soon as I pull her out of her seat, she's already dashing toward the entrance. "Hailey!" I holler after her, remotely locking my car while catching up with her and taking her hand with mine. "Don't run off, okay?"

"I'm just so excited!"

I grin. I know I shouldn't. I should lecture her on how dangerous it can be running in a parking lot, but damn those blue eyes and blond curls . . . The kid is just too damn cute. "Okay. Just be careful. Hold my hand."

She agrees, and we walk inside. We're greeted by the principal—an older, but friendly woman who directs us to Hailey's new classroom, which we find easily. When we walk inside, I'm suddenly frozen in place, struck by the sight of the hottest man I've ever seen.

I stare.

Hailey squeals as she looks around.

The man stands with a bright smile on his handsome face. He probably has a year or two on me, but he's still pretty young. His light brown hair is perfectly trimmed and styled, cut short on the sides but with thick waves on top. He has a manicured, short beard that is immaculate. And his eyes . . .

*Fuck, his eyes.*

They actually sparkle. I've heard of that but always thought it was bullshit. But his brown eyes? Yeah, they have little flecks of gold that actually sparkle when he smiles. Which so far, has been always.

We're about the same height, although he might have an inch or two on me. And he's broad-chested, stretching out his crisp lavender button-down to the max. His muscles strain against the sleeves, and I can't shake the thought of wanting to see him out of his starched, perfectly fitting dress clothes.

He clears his throat and holds his large hand out for mine. "I'm Mr. Burke."

"Mister?" My brain finally catches up, and I can feel my eyes widening. "Mister Burke?"

"Yes," he says, his lips curling with amusement. "I'm sorry about the mix-up. I know the enrollment form said 'Miss.'"

"You're a boy," Hailey says next to me, and I can't tell if she's sad or happy about that fact.

*Me?*

*Yeah, I'd rather it was a "Miss" and not an insanely hot "Mister."*

Once again, the universe is fucking with me. I clear my throat and shake his hand firmly. "I'm Rafe Scott. You can call me Rafe though."

He smiles and nods politely, releasing my hand. "Okay. Then you must be Hailey, right?" He looks down at my daughter with a fondness I didn't expect.

I know it's sexist, but I never saw a male kindergarten teacher coming. "Yup! I'm Hailey Eileen Scott."

Mr. Burke grins at her and holds his hand out, leaning down so they're eye level. "Well, it's great to meet you, Miss Hailey." She giggles, but her eyes are scoping out the classroom and not her new teacher. Unlike her father, who cannot make himself look away. He's still crouched down at her eye level although he's released her hand. "How would you like to play with some of the cool toys we have here while I talk to your dad about boring stuff?"

"Yes!" She bounces off, not needing another invitation.

Mr. Burke directs me to a small table and two ridiculously small chairs. "Sit?"

I stare at the chair. "You kidding?"

He chuckles. "I promise, a chair has never given way on me. You'll be fine." He takes a seat in one of the tiny chairs, and I shrug, taking a seat across from him.

He pulls out a folder full of papers with Hailey's name on it and starts going over some of the basics, mostly a mission statement for the year.

"So, this will be her first year in school?"

I nod. "Yeah. She was with my aunt last year. I didn't think she'd need preschool." I grip the back of my neck, suddenly embarrassed that I let my kid down or something.

"Not a problem." He doesn't seem to be judging me.

"She's really smart." I have no idea why I feel the need to defend my decisions. "And I uh, worked nights. So I wouldn't have seen her at all."

Those brown eyes meet mine with curiosity but again, no judgment. "Makes sense." He looks down at the papers in front of him. "And will she be riding the bus? Or will you be dropping off and picking up?"

"The bus in the morning. My aunt's friend, well, her daughter— she's going to be putting Hailey on the bus for me because I go to work at five, but I'll be there to pick her up every afternoon."

He nods, and I wish I could just shut up. I've never had a problem with being quiet before, but something about him unsettles me. Like I need to defend myself. "That's perfectly fine. I just need to know so I don't put her on the bus in the afternoon."

"I'll be here." I give him the clipped answer and feel like a dick. That part, I'm used to. Most people assume I'm an asshole from the get-go, and I suppose I can be one.

"Can I ask about her mother?"

My body stiffens. My eyes immediately go to Hailey, who is playing happily across the room.

Every instinct inside me is saying no.

But I know that he's only asking because he's going to be her teacher. He should know her background.

*No matter how painful.*

**Totally Schooled is also free with Kindle Unlimited and available on Amazon!**

Totally Schooled - Kindle edition by Dykes, Nicole. Literature & Fiction Kindle eBooks @ Amazon.com.

# STALKER LINKS

Website:

https://www.authornicoledykes.com

Facebook:

https://www.facebook.com/Author-Nicole-D-
1607194522867504/

Facebook MM Reads Group:

https://www.facebook.com/groups/4668034456620878

Instagram:

https://www.instagram.com/nicoledauthor/

Amazon:

https://www.amazon.com/Nicole-Dykes/e/B01D1SIF04/

Goodreads:

https://www.goodreads.com/author/show/
13701591.Nicole_Dykes

Bookbub:

https://www.bookbub.com/profile/nicole-dykes

Made in the USA
Las Vegas, NV
02 February 2022

42791358R00132